SOMETHING
OF
THE NIGHT

SOMETHING
OF
THE NIGHT

MARY McMULLEN

PUBLISHED FOR THE CRIME CLUB BY
DOUBLEDAY & COMPANY, INC.
GARDEN CITY, NEW YORK
1980

To my sister Katherine

All of the characters in this book
are fictitious, and any resemblance
to actual persons, living or dead,
is purely coincidental.

ISBN: 0-385-17182-X
Library of Congress Catalog Card Number 80–1035
Copyright © 1980 by Doubleday & Company, Inc.
All Rights Reserved
Printed in the United States of America
First Edition

ONE

The letter from Markie, if you could call it a letter, was bad enough.

For two days, Kells Cavanaugh tried to rationalize it, stomach it—dismiss it.

A lined sheet of yellowish paper torn from a ringbound pad, the top edge raggedy. A drawing obviously done in haste, in crayons, the strokes swift and oddly lifelike: a tiger, its stripes dashed in, but with a lion's mane and slanted devouring eyes, not dark but pale.

He was a bright child and could print, if somewhat large and crookedly. "This is Ian, Mr. Milford. Please don't let him. Please please please daddy don't LET THEM. From, your son Markie."

He must have managed it behind Bridget's back. She wouldn't let such a communication cross the Atlantic unexplained. Secretly making off with a snatched piece of paper, stealing or say helping himself to an airmail stamp, 12p, and to an envelope of expensive heavy creamy paper.

"Whether you like it or not, Kells, you're to lunch at the Four Seasons with your radial-tire people. Or one of them." His secretary, Etheldred, was a noticeable girl but he hadn't been aware of her coming into his large sunlit corner office. "Are you all right? Has someone turned something down? You look a bit off-color."

He had had a late night and gotten up late, picking up his mail from the lobby box to take along to his place of employment, Cavanaugh and Cavanaugh, Inc. It was past eleven now. Markie's letter was the first one he had opened.

Etheldred was Welsh, tall, fair, rosy and windblown even in quiet enclosed spaces. A sensible girl. If shown the note, she would smile and say, "Well, normal, I'd think. Who'd want a new father when they already have you?"

If, that is, she knew about Caroline's plans. But she didn't. He was by nature a private man and in addition to this he thought it wouldn't do to get too close, too easy, with Etheldred; she was charming and would, he felt, be available. His, dear God, office wife.

"I thought Gerald was going to take on the tires." Gerald Cavanaugh was his older brother, founder of the small, selective, and notably successful advertising agency. After ten years at Y and R, Kells had bought in and doubled the firm name. Gerald was the writer of the family, Kells the artist. He was comfortably titled and placed at the head of the art department, where the name and talents he brought with him rocked only a few very ambitious boats.

"Gerald had to take a morning plane to Atlanta, swearing all the way. He's left you a bundle of memos to bone up on."

He wanted to look at the letter again but didn't dare under the near observing eyes. He remembered now two or three coinlike spots on the printing, dried. Tears. Running down to the nose corners, to the chin, and then falling on the paper.

"I suppose Hichens will come along to help?" Hichens was the account man on Continental Tires. A sudden recollection—

Hichens had been divorced last year. He had three children, two boys and a girl. His ex-wife too was about to remarry.

"Yes, he'll meet you there. And now off to the conference room with you, Burghold's Beer meeting. There are pitchers of it—refilled—up and down the table. Everybody's been nipping."

Cab at twelve-thirty to Seagram House, one of his favorite New York Buildings, dark and mighty in the October sunlight. Fast walk between the terrace fountains, into the Four

Seasons restaurant, turn right at the Picasso tapestry into the bar, nod at the waiting Hichens, take a stool beside him.

The gold-beaded garlands of the Miró curtains flashed at the immensely tall windows; a reflection from his glass struck Hichens' pleasant homely face. He looked like a prosperous farmer, and clients from the midwest found this reassuring.

"Dunbar makes a practice of being exactly fifteen minutes late," he said. "Martini?"

"Then why don't you always turn up fifteen minutes late?"

"I did, just once, and the bastard was right on the dot for the first and only time in his life."

In an abrupt way quite unlike him, Kells asked without preforming the question in his mind, "Are you having any trouble with your kids? New father and so on?" He might not have broached the subject to another man, but he liked Hichens.

Hichens laughed, a little sourly. "Christ, they're crazy about him, at least so far. The boys anyway. He's a big sports man, plays touch football with them, all I hear when they come to pay a visit is how great Reg is, Daddy."

"Oh."

"Why?"

"Nothing," Kells said. "Just a passing thought."

Another drink with Dunbar, a gray thin faceless man who wanted advice on whether to switch his commercials from the "Today Show" to the "Tonight Show." ("Actually because," Hichens explained privately later, "his wife sleeps through 'Today' and always watches 'Tonight' and bedevils him about spending all that money on commercials no one ever sees.")

Lamb chops, creamed potatoes, minted green peas. Hichens with consummate offhand skill planting the idea of *both* Today and Tonight. "After all, you're one of the giants, why not just stride into top position?"

Dunbar the giant, mellowed with two manhattans and plentiful wine, producing a picture from his wallet, his ten-year-old son. "Any kiddies of your own, Kells? I don't know why, but you look to me like a bachelor."

"Yes. One."

"Got a picture on you? To compare notes and noses?"

"Sorry, I haven't." Picture in his head, the flying hand with the crayons, the tears, trickling, slow. Somewhere where he was alone, where Bridget wouldn't see what he was up to.

He heard himself talking quite sensibly, the details having been quickly digested during his cab ride, about the new flight of tire commercials while Caroline's letter repeated itself in an inner ear. It had come two days ago. He hadn't answered it yet.

". . . I'm sure you're not particularly interested in his appearance and charms, so let us get to practical things. Quite solid financially, as far as I can gather, runs one of those blue-chip real estate affairs like our Previews, Inc. Mansions in Barbados and vast country properties and town houses on the most expensive and elegant streets and squares in London. Their name is Pruitt and Cream, the firm is apparently over a hundred years old, solid as one of Mr. Landseer's Trafalgar lions.

"Married before, ten years back. His wife died when they were living in Rhodesia, in Salisbury. One thinks of divorce, ours, as sad and racking, but it's a picnic compared to the real, awful loss."

Her handwriting was rounded and small. He could see her browsing over her letter, seated at some pretty writing desk in Anne's house. Looking as always like a portrait from another century. Music to be heard in the background, she liked music in the air about her. Head bent to her task, the serenely center-parted soft brown hair falling loosely forward around the pale delicate blue-eyed face.

"Your first concern, naturally, will not be about me but about Markie. And to repeat a useful word, naturally Markie is a little miffed, a little jealous I suppose, someone else entering the ménage. He wouldn't be normal if he didn't feel that way. There were no children of the previous marriage and Ian is quite looking forward to having a son and being a father. He's an Englishman, by the way, in case I haven't put that down, and I hardly need add a gentleman. The family originally from somewhere in the West Riding, and his grandfather was a bishop, *the* famous Bishop Milford, except that I'd never heard of him and probably neither have you."

Yes, it was a useful word and way of looking at things. Naturally Caroline would not choose to remain single indefinitely. She had had her freedom for two years now and would want her own household, her own linens and silver and china, and the pleasant sight for all the world to see, of her being chosen, necessary to the life of a man.

Naturally—in spite of Hichens' oddball children—Markie would resent the newcomer, the intruder. Naturally, he would present the man to his real father as a snake, or a great green beetle, or a tiger with a lion's mane. Momentary rejection, dislike, expressed with a child's forthright simplicity.

"By the way, it's all rather a secret, so don't tell everybody, I'll surprise them with announcements. And now I must finish this up, the three of us are off to Regent's Park zoo, it's a lovely day for lion and elephant gazing. About the wedding, I think perhaps within the month, toward the end, although in the manner of the male Ian keeps saying 'Why not tomorrow?' By the way, Kells, whenever you brush your teeth *always* remember to rinse with one-half teaspoon of salt in four inches of warm water. I got this advice at immense expense from a Mayfair periodontist and I pass it along to you absolutely free. I hope you're well but then you always seem to be. Affectionately, Caroline."

Had something happened at the zoo? A threatening hiss behind a hand while Caroline was otherwise occupied, perhaps admiring the magnificent display of dahlias near the elephant house? A man bent on a new love, and having to choke down a small boy, a present enemy, as part of the package?

He was grateful in the afternoon for the hard deadline work on Burghold's Beer waiting for him at his drawing board. During negotiations a year ago, he had said, "I must work, you know, Gerald. I wasn't born to sit and officiate."

"Why do you think I'm letting you blast your good money on this place? So, work," said Gerald.

Buying in, after long persuasion from his brother, assuming the top position he was quietly aware he well deserved, wasn't a matter of management drive, or thundering ego. Kells had learned early enough that if you hadn't climbed a height of some authority you could have inferior brains and talents squatting heavily on your back.

"No no, Kells, nice try but that isn't the way I see it at all. Now, how about *this* approach?" And someone else's neuroses, fears, ambitions, thumb-twitchings and head-scratching to guide you, force you on your daily way.

He fastidiously avoided competition with his staff of art directors; he had his own block of accounts and invaded no other unless help was needed. His professional presence was amiable and low-key, yet underscored with a crackle of excitement which would have come as news to him. He was a shy man and to compensate for this gave every evidence of ease and swift responsiveness.

Tempting idea, work late, finish the job tonight, and then fall into bed too tired to think or worry about anything. But no, save some of it for tomorrow, a sure and clear way to avoid sitting in for Gerald at detested meetings and conferences.

It would have been helpful to be able to talk to Gerald.

"For God's sake, Kells! What do you expect, a portrait of the man with a halo around it? Markie is merely reacting like any other red-blooded American brat. What you need is a drink followed by another drink."

He went home and took Gerald's advice.

The following afternoon he did what he now thought he ought to have done after he opened the letter, the tiger letter. Four o'clock here, nine there. Markie would be safely in bed.

He called Anne Eldredge's house in London. If Caroline answered, "Hello, I got your letter and I thought I'd call rather than write."

By luck, it was Bridget Dorsey's voice.

"Hello, Bridget. Sorry to sound mysterious but if there are people around would you mind finding a phone where you can't be listened to and call me back as soon as possible? You have my office number."

"Yes, all right, Kells. Give me a few minutes," said efficient, reliable Bridget.

And then she proceeded to perpetrate what from his end seemed an act of astonishing inefficiency.

There were four telephones in the house. One in the kitchen; one in the entrance hall, in a closet under the stairs behind a canework door; one on the stair landing outside the door of Bridget's room; and the fourth, new, on the table beside Caroline's bed.

Bridget found herself without any great doubt about the reason for Kells' transatlantic call. She stood in her open bedroom doorway for a moment, listening. The door into Markie's room was slightly ajar. Silence.

Ian Milford, in her mental eye, was sitting sprawled on one of the facing love seats at the hearth before the fire, drinking brandy and impatiently glancing at his watch, waiting for Caroline to come home from a literary cocktail party in Clerkenwell's Green. Anne would be deep in her tub with a volume of Dickens propped on the reading tray.

Murmuring could be more attention-catching than speaking normally; no, not the phone on the landing. Use Caroline's? It would be unattractive to be caught secretly occupying her room. And in any case the impatient Ian might stride to the hall, pick up the phone in the closet to demand Caroline's return from her party, and find the line engaged, most interestingly engaged.

The box on the corner would be best. It was a mild night, no coat needed. She went down the long angled stairway and past the open double doors of the drawing room without looking in.

Anne's house commanded the end of a short cul-de-sac,

Emlyn Court. The house faced toward Sloane Avenue, an ample and graceful Palladian structure which with its size and position made the double row of little carriage houses at right angles to it along the court look like attendant beings. The red telephone box was in front of the pale green house on the corner.

Kells answered after one ring. "Tell me anything that comes into your head about Ian Milford." No explanations or apologies. With Bridget they wouldn't be needed.

She felt immediately tongue-tied. But that wouldn't do, not with the cost of this phone call. "A handsome man, very. Tall, sure of himself, knows his way around, seems well in funds."

"*Bridget.*"

"He's obviously not used to the company of young children and will have to feel his way a bit—overdoes it sometimes, underdoes it other times." Be cautious, feel *your* way here. Other people's business, don't grind your heel on it. "You know how Markie feels about you. That would almost explain . . ." Stop.

"Explain what?"

Because she was a little troubled on and off, and had been for several months; and because it was he, very far but very near, she said on a long breath without thinking it out beforehand, "Perhaps there is something of the night about him—"

A short silence. Then, "For Christ's sake, Bridget, don't go Irish and mystic on me. Markie's obviously frightened of or by him, I got a letter which he must have sneaked past you. Would you say like everybody else that it's a normal, passing thing? Just be patient, everybody?"

The center-hinged door of the box exploded outward. A small bathrobed body flung itself against her side.

"*It's him it's him it's daddy isn't it?* I heard you say his name and I went down the back stairs and through the garden and came after you."

"What the *hell* is going on?" demanded Kells in her ear.

"Oh . . . Markie's here with me." She severely regretted the slipped-out "something of the night." Now, when and how had that entered her head? "I'm sorry I have nothing concrete to offer you about—mmm—Mr. Lawson. Given the one person, and ten observers, you'll get ten different opinions."

Usually well-mannered, Markie was reaching frantically for the phone. "Let me, let me talk to him please?"

"You have just lost a stripe, Bridget," Kells said. "Oh well, put him on."

A confused, "Hello, Daddy, are you all the way over there —" and then at the sound of his father's voice an eruption of tears, shoulders bent and all his body shaking. Through the sobbing, a few raw syllables. "Please . . . please . . . I *told* you . . . in my letter . . ."

A scream across an ocean.

For help?

". . . a normal red-blooded American brat." Markie wasn't a brat, or hadn't been last he'd seen him, three months ago.

Or something in between the two extremes: I'm worried and upset, I'm lost, for now. Will you straighten things out for me? Please?

"Calm down, Markie. It just happens that I have business in London and I'll see you in—"

Hard to remember what day it was when you were all but torn to pieces. Tuesday.

"I'll see you Thursday. And now you might like to remind Bridget that it's well past your bedtime."

TWO

"Who, what, and why is Bridget?" Anne Eldredge had asked upon first seeing her, shortly after the divorce. "I mean, obviously not a nanny. Although quite nice—rather a lady, would you say?"

Bridget had entered the Cavanaugh domestic circle a year before that. They were staying, during a European journey—the final attempt on Kells' part to try to salvage a marriage that wasn't working—with his cousin Maud in Killiney, high over the Irish Sea. Caroline had gone off on an impromptu picnic with Maud's young brother Dermot, and had been having such a good time that she forgot about Markie and lost him, or rather let him lose himself. He was found after four frightful hours of searching.

While she enjoyed and loved her son, she had often chafed under the burden of his daily care. "I can't be expected to give up all my friends and all my fun and sit from morning till night and *stare* at him. And those girls—what? three to date?—are all on speed or pot or worse, and will stay only a few months or so, you just can't find reliable help anymore."

Carefully containing himself on this occasion, because if he blew he would blow his world right down around his ears, Kells went to Maud for assistance. It would be nice, he said, if they could find someone, some pleasant responsible young woman, to take care of Markie on a permanent basis. "Caroline naturally doesn't like to be cabined and confined. Someone who for a reasonable salary wouldn't mind leaving the country."

"Let me think," said Maud. Peg Lavery and her husband

the doctor were guests at the house too. Peg knew everybody. In this nation of cousins, Peg turned out to have one she thought might do.

She always thought of Bridget Dorsey as poor Bridget, and the girl occasionally weighed on her conscience. After all, what utter rotten luck. The parents, young and attractive, killed in a road accident when she was five. Then off to the care of her mother's considerably older, unmarried sister Della. Bridget wanting to be an artist, but instead sent off to nursing school.

"There's money in nursing," said sour Della. "People do get sick all the time. And you never saw, speaking of that, an undertaker go hungry, did you?"

After a year at St. Augusta's College, the money ran out. Della shortly afterward fell ill and, turn and turn about, she became the care of Bridget.

Possible suitors were swiftly aware that along with Bridget would come Della, on a silver platter. Bed and all.

There were the usual dreary jobs available to the untrained. The last, best paid, and dreariest of all was the greeting card company, Donahue and Sons. She had had no formal training in art but had a good deal of undeveloped talent and got to be looked upon as a prize by the senior Donahue.

Birthday cards, Christmas, Easter, Mother's Day and Father's Day. Cards for the newborn and the newly bereaved by death. Ordination and First Communion, anniversaries, graduation, get well.

At first, Bridget tried a few what she considered good things, fresh and surprising. She was shortly forced to give up this approach. The cards were aimed with deadly accuracy, low. A low learned the hard way, as Mr. Donahue tossed aside anything smacking of taste.

"People who have taste write letters. They're not our crowd. Mary Ann, I like this crucifix. What would you say to one perfect, crystal tear rolling down somewhere about the center of the upright?"

The all-time best-seller was the "Weeping Child" card. It was sent for funerals, and other family emergencies; but it was mainly used by people to scold other people for whatever off-the-path matters they were up to.

It was while the staff was working on Granda's Day that Della finally died.

("One up on the Americans!" cried Mr. Donahue. "Dear old grandfather! Mind you, boys and girls, no old fellows sitting in the corner by the ashes. No spitting, snoring, or bottle-tilting.")

After the funeral, Bridget took a week off from Granda. "Right and proper," Mr. Donahue said. "A sad loss," and had a terrible job to keep from winking.

Della hadn't owned the house and left no money and no possessions of any value; but now only about half as much money would be needed. Peg after leaving the graveside said, "Are you going to stay on at that ghastly job?" "I don't know," said Bridget. "Leave it and find another ghastly job?"

She was then twenty-six. Three days before she was to go back to work—*if* she could bear to go back to Donahue and Sons—Peg called her from Killiney.

"I know it sounds strange, Brid, but it might be a tub of butter. After all, you've a year of nurse's training, you'd be on a semiprofessional basis. And you'd be yanked right out of your horrid little rut, up and away like the birds. She's—Mrs. Cavanaugh—rather lovely and he's awfully nice. And the little boy is a bit of a dear. Think of it, the States and probably some traveling, they don't seem short of money."

Bridget took a bus to Killiney and was interviewed by Kells. He informed her that Mrs. Cavanaugh was in Dublin shopping but she soon found that she, a person to be with Markie, steadily with him, was the father's idea and the father's concern.

After about four minutes he decided she was exactly right, and had never since had occasion to change his mind. There was something, in the old and not contemporary meaning of the word, reassuringly square about her. Square face, broad oblong of forehead, square white teeth, the upper ones slightly protruding, gently lifting her lip. Grave hazel eyes, large, and plainly cut short dark hair. She had an air of quiet strength, not aggressive but encircling her in her own zone. Her build was short, firm and sturdy.

(I wish, Bridget said to herself while being politely but thoroughly examined by the gray eyes, that out of boredom and Della and spinstering around Dublin I hadn't allowed myself to put on an extra fifteen pounds.)

They reached a rapid agreement. Try it for six months, and if it worked out probably a job of four years or so; Markie was then three. "I wonder," Bridget said, "why you wouldn't prefer an American?"

"I thought an Irish girl would be less expensive and, I don't know, more reliable," Kells said. "You don't mind traveling a bit before we head home? Two weeks in Italy, wandering around by car, a week in London?"

"Not at all." The faint smile showed two startling dimples.

Her salary was to be eight thousand dollars a year. "And all found," added Kells, bursting out laughing. "Forgive me, but I'm new to personnel work. How soon can you start?"

"Shouldn't the child look me over?"

"No. I'm well acquainted with him and our tastes aren't unlike."

She sat for a moment considering. "Three days. No, two. You'll still be here on the Friday?"

"Yes, until Sunday." Immediately and delicately establishing a relationship-to-be, positioning employer and employee, he said, "And now let's go and find your cousin Peg and have a drink on it, shall we?"

"Well really, Kells," Caroline said. "You might at least have shown her to me."

"Question of snapping her up before she changed her mind," Kells said. "I think she's what used to be called in the dear dead days a jewel."

There was never any discussion of uniform, but Bridget tactfully settled it for herself by ordering three new suits, navy, brown, and gray, with pleated skirts and double-breasted box jackets buttoned in pearl. They were neither demure nor sexy, but easy, trim, and comfortable.

Caroline, prepared to criticize, was pleased by the fair fresh skin, no makeup that she could discern, and the soft clear voice, only a trace of Irish accent. It wouldn't do, she thought, to have Markie pick up a brogue. With that squareish figure and scrubbed face and quiet manner—was it what used to be known as dignity?—she could be comfortably dismissed as another *woman*, a potential rival at one's own hearth.

Peg was fascinated by what she had wrought. "Are you a governess? Or nursemaid? Or what? Do they call you Dorsey?"

"A kind of companion, as far as I can gather. No teaching unless I decide to amuse myself at it. They call me Bridget."

"Do you have to do his wash and cook his meals?"

"No, but I might take over the food."

"Will you dine with them?"

"I will not. Probably with Markie or in my room or both, my Della days drove me into a hopeless habit of reading with dinner after I brought up her tray."

"And," Peg giggled, "are you allowed, what's the word, followers?"

"I understand that I do more or less what I like," Bridget said a little starchily. "As long as I take Markie off their hands. Hers, rather. Although they seem very fond of each other, she and the boy. She likes him in the English way, delivered clean and brushed, late in the afternoon. Or being dazzled when she comes in to kiss him goodnight, all furs and scent before going out."

"Dear God, New York in a few weeks, and a lovely place it is no matter what the papers say. The Museum of Modern Art, the Metropolitan—*what* a wallow you'll have—the theater and the opera and the ballet. The shops, and Rockefeller Center, such fun to hear the 'Skaters Waltz' floating along

Fifth Avenue from the rink. What did I tell you about a tub of butter?"

She and Markie had taken a fortunate and early fancy to each other. He was a small thin child with fashionably cut tow-colored hair falling into his gentle wide gray gaze and tumbling around his cheeks and nape. With comely parents, his looks were all but guaranteed; but it was something more, something of the spirit, that went to her heart.

"He'll be brown, or black, at about eight, my brother and I were, even though we started out this way," Kells said, lightly fingering the tow hair. As a father, he seemed to Bridget to have a kind of European ease and grace; he showed no self-consciousness, hearty brusqueness, or fist-feinting in his open affection for his son.

Three days after she started work, Markie demanded anxiously of him, "Will Bridget be here next week? next month? next year?" worrying about her to the furthest infinity of time.

"Yes, and for years more, if she likes us."

At the end of the six months, Kells said, "You'll stay on, won't you? Obviously you're more than ever needed now."

Bridget, not a willing listener or watcher, was unable to avoid the sad sounds and sight of a marriage falling apart.

Nor to arrive at her own shadowy conclusions concerning the scenario. Not only Caroline's looks to net him, four years back, but something softly, bendingly helpless about her, a projected eager need for the strength of another.

Before she could be stopped, a woman who came in to cook for dinner parties, a Mrs. Eames, said while stirring her béchamel sauce, "I heard her tell him, all sighs and murmurs —it must have been about the end of the first year—that she'd been hopelessly in love with someone when she met him and that he was getting her nicely over it. If you could have heard the silence thundering out of him, although he's quite a pleasant man usually. . . ."

The lost love had divorced his wife and, free again, would

turn up as a dinner guest or invite Caroline to lunch. But then, she had a great many men friends; she said most women were tiresome creatures. There was nothing overt, no sign of physical imprudence or misbehavior; she needed her circle of admiration, her warm male hearth.

Kells seemed to stand a little outside the circle, watching her without comment. A flash of intuition told Bridget that perhaps at bottom his trouble was that, now, she bored him.

It was Caroline, she thought, who must have finally demanded the divorce. It was clear to her that Caroline could not stand failure.

The apartment, the ominously calm battleground, was in the East Seventies. She kept Markie out of it—out of the atmosphere of a void, a silence, a clock that had stopped ticking —as much as possible. Kells' work, mainly television commercials for Cavanaugh and Cavanaugh's clients Pan-Globe Airways and Spa Intercontinental Hotels, took him away a good deal. Sent him to the coast, to São Paulo in Brazil, to New Orleans, Banff, Paris, and London. It occurred to her that he probably welcomed the faraway jobs; was in a position, even, to initiate them. When in New York, the pressure of work seemed to claim him and he often turned up well after midnight.

He had someone to solace him, she supposed. Caroline in one way or another had asked for it.

In due course she was informed of the custody arrangements.

"Nine months with Caroline, three with me," Kells said. "I could have managed a six-months split but I thought that might almost literally slice him in half. He's got to have some continuity. Thank God you provide the better part of that."

Peg heard about the divorce from Kells' cousin Maud. She wrote and asked, "What will this do to your job? Do you propose, minx, to spend months alone with him in an apartment? And just a bit of a child to chaperone you?"

Her romantic imaginings were given no fuel to feed on. "Yes, I do," answered Bridget. "And do you think it would be scandalous to leave him alone with a washing machine, or a refrigerator, or any other household equipment?"

For Markie's sake, she got on easily and well with Caroline, but she was—how to put it to herself?—extremely fond of Kells. She was aware that any psychiatrist would have told her that she was probably wiping out her own normal future as a wife, or partner, or mother, by fixating, yes, that would be the word the psychiatrist would use, on somebody else's child. But willy-nilly she loved Markie. And, in for a penny in for a pound.

THREE

Kells woke to a brief green contentment in his room at the Hyde Park Hotel. The green was color reflected on the pale walls from trees and grass, and the contentment was the thank-you of a mind and body carried over the Atlantic in a 747 after a full hard day's work in New York.

Grateful for the cool linen sheets, he blinked at the ceiling with the usual where-am-I question of the traveler first waking in another country.

"Planes that pass in the night," he had said to Gerald, having a quick drink with him in Gerald's big shadowy office before taking a cab to Kennedy to the British Airways terminal.

Gerald had just gotten in from Atlanta, where he had managed to salvage for the third time the slippery thirty-million-dollar Lola-Cola account.

He didn't speak any of the lines Kells had written for him. Shown the letter from Markie and informed of the telephone explosion, he said, "Of course, go, what else can you do?"

He was terrified of flying and could only cope with it on quantities of martinis, which might have accounted for the vividness of his reactions.

"Ian Milford. Sounds like a cad, doesn't he?" As the brother older by three years, larger, and more vehement, he gave every evidence of having thought up this project by himself.

"Different if he was an American, and if and when you were worried you could run over to their apartment and take Markie's pulse. But he'll probably be living in England most of the year. Unless this chap's planning a world cruise, or several, on Caroline's money."

He poured another drink for both of them. "House agent, did she say?"

"On a grand scale, I gather."

"For all you know," Gerald propounded extravagantly, "he could be a dealer in narcotics, or an international jewel thief, or some such thing. Or in other kinds of ways an unsuitable father for Markie." Kells was not amused as his fancy continued its flight. "A pervert of some kind, or a smooth crook . . . Caroline's bad at choosing the right men for her."

"Thank you," said Kells.

"Well, it's your plain duty as his father to see what she's getting them into. Of course you won't let her know why you've shot to London like a bat out of hell, they might immediately try to cover things up if there's anything to cover. And naturally, she might be a bit angry about the detective work on your part— Let me think."

He went to the window wall and looked out at rainswept city lights in the early dark.

"Officially, you're there to put in a spell of work on something or other—say, Bonar's Bread, or whatever you please." Kells had thought all this out for himself but listened patiently. "They'll have an office for you—make way, everybody, for the vice-president and junior partner. There's as a matter of fact a little trouble there, sounds like petty office nonsense to me but you might look into it. I have a letter somewhere in the desk."

Tall and rumpled, thick dark hair untidy, he sat at his desk owlishly peering at envelopes, and then buzzed for his secretary. It was seven o'clock, but she was still there. He took the sketchiest of notes on business trips and would soon be dictating to her for an hour or so, wearily but colorfully. "And for Christ's sake leave out the blasphemies, Maura dear."

"Here's the London letter," Maura said, finding it instantly. "Reservations all taken care of, Kells? Would you like a limo?"

"There is no such word in the English language as limo,"

Gerald said, scowling fiercely at her. Kells said thanks but a cab would do.

"Well, I'll see that one's kept waiting at the door for you, mustn't get wet, I do like that suit."

All the secretaries at Cavanaugh and Cavanaugh were college-degreed and planned very brief stops behind their typewriters before going on to juicier careers there.

"Have a drink, Maura." Seeing Kells glance at his watch, he said, "One more thought for you. There's a girl at the London office, Maisie Tombs, a very interesting girl"—sounding reminiscent and a little regretful—"who goes everywhere and knows everybody. Mad, but then so many of the English are. She might have run across this Milford bounder at one of her parties. In any case, she's worth cultivating. And *you* have nothing to stop you, damn it."

This last was probably a rakish touch for Maura's benefit; Gerald was happily married with three young children of his own.

"Actually," Maura would say to Kells' secretary Etheldred, "Kells is Gerald *corrected*. His parents spotted a few slips—a nose here, an eyebrow there—and set out to produce a superior model."

"I like craggy men," Etheldred defended. "And anyway what good is it? Nobody can make a dent in Kells. I should know."

As Kells got up to go, Gerald characteristically began to reverse himself.

"All that gin and vermouth and I were probably just amusing ourselves. He may be a paragon, a pillar of the community. No, they don't, thank God, have communities in England, I hate the term. Or he could be a dedicated leader of the Boy Scouts on his weekends, poor Markie. You're not, I assume, going to dither about indefinitely there, seeing if his fingerprints are on record and so on? We have a hell of a lot of work to do on the cola, everything's down the drain, six new commercials staring us in the face."

"I'll make it as quick as possible," Kells said. "Of course I have no idea what I'm getting into. As you say, probably nothing. Nothing at all."

Knowing that to Markie Thursday meant *Thursday*, from the moment he woke at a no doubt impossibly early hour, he called Anne's house from Heathrow. His eyes felt as though they had been starched. It was seven-thirty.

Bridget answered, speaking not to him at first but voice left. ". . . Yes, Markie, just a moment. Hello? Oh good, it's you, he's been up since five. I'll put him on."

Yes, Kells assured Markie, he was here. *Where?* Heathrow, you remember Heathrow. He was going now to his hotel to get a few hours' sleep and would call again later. Today? Yes, today. Before lunch? Yes, before lunch. He would see him soon, very soon.

He put himself back at the age of six and remembered that soon could be forever.

"Your mother's asleep, I suppose?" Yes, she was. Thank God. With his head about to float away with him, he didn't want to take on Caroline at the moment.

Why, he wondered, as he showered and dressed after waking at eleven, this feeling of eggshell-walking? A simple matter, really, now that he was here. See what Milford was like, reassure Markie, check in at the office, perhaps tomorrow.

No, today. Caroline might call there to see that his *i*'s were properly dotted and be told that, no, Mr. Cavanaugh hadn't been in touch with them, was he expected?

Rested and braced, he was ready for Caroline. "Kells. I'd like to say what a nice surprise but Markie has been driving us all mad with the countdown. Markie, be *quiet—*"

He explained his presence, some work to supervise at the Allory Place office. "But first I'll come around and pick up Markie for lunch, or anyway take him somewhere." Don't sound too confident of your claim, your position. "If that's all right."

Slight hesitation, hinting at possible inconvenience or complications. "Oh dear," Caroline said. "Sorry to sound—but *just* at this time." The rest of it hung unspoken in the air. Just when Markie's getting used to the idea of his other father. "Mmmm . . . well, I suppose— But you know it will mean a bit of a shakeup, although of course as long as you're *here* you can't very well . . ."

The softest of slaps, gentlest of pinches: You know what it will do to him, seeing you here, seeing you leave, right in the middle of otherwise perfect peace and quiet.

One of his eggshells crunched noisily under his foot.

He called Cavanaugh and Cavanaugh, Inc., got the receptionist, Miss King, and told her he'd be by later in the day. Then he went out into the fine early-October sunlight and stood for a moment on the steps positioning himself. The hotel offered a meeting of roads, Knightsbridge, Brompton, and Sloane Street. It had been years since he had wandered Chelsea on foot, with Caroline. "But you've spent practically half your life there, are you sure that's what you want for your wedding trip?" "Yes," said Caroline. "I want to show you off from Cheyne Walk to the King's Road."

Caroline's mother Cecelia had married the American John Wintergate, and died when Caroline was seven years old. Cecelia's unmarried older sister Anne had become like a casual on-and-off second mother to her. Caroline spent her summers with her aunt, and had had several school years in England; she had grown up a native of two countries.

"And we must keep it up," she told Kells. "It's not only that I have to have my time there, part of me is in London and down in the country, in Sussex. But—not to grub money but no point in looking away from it—if we have children they'll probably inherit. She has no one else, no blood relatives that is."

He had been a little taken aback by this farsighted practical note. Caroline had plenty of money of her own from her mother and from her father, who had been a five-star corporation lawyer.

She and Markie had been visiting Anne for three months now; or rather living there comfortably, in her other land.

Emlyn Court couldn't be more than a half mile away. After six hours on the plane, and the taxi ride from Heathrow, crawling in heavy going-to-work traffic, and the spell in bed, his legs wanted stretching. He chose the Brompton Road and cut through Harrods, pausing to buy flowers for Anne, yellow roses, and a handsome toy sailboat for Markie. He emerged on Walton Street at the back and by pleasant trial and error, in a skein of crescents and lanes, streets and squares, he found Emlyn Court in twenty minutes.

There must have been a long anxious window-watch. The front door burst open and Markie came pelting down the narrow cobble-stoned court between the parked cars. From a distance of several feet away, he flung himself at Kells, who fielded him with one arm, maintaining a precarious hold with the other on his Harrods packages. No tears, no pent-up terrors here and now, but radiance and only the slightest quiver, of flesh expressing joy.

A pour of chatter, interrupted with "How long will you be here, for a week, for a month?"

"For a while," Kells answered comfortably, holding the small hand as they walked to the open door. "Let's go find your aunt, and where is your mother?"

"Dressing, to go out."

"And Bridget?"

"Sewing on buttons."

Tactful Bridget, leaving them alone.

Inside the door, in the broad walnut-paneled hall, one of two mynah birds in a bamboo cage uttered a shrill wolf whistle at the sight of Kells and said, "Good news, good news, good news." Anne had trained him into this pronouncement, thinking it would be nice for arriving guests. The house was full of caged birds, the mynahs and parrots, macaws, canaries, finches, the pale blue and buff and the brilliantly colored Australian, lovebirds and cockatoos.

Anne Eldredge herself, at sixty, bore a certain resemblance

to her birds. She was a short square-shouldered woman with a high, polished, beaky nose, her skin a color somewhere between rose and maghogany from her year-round exposure to the elements. Her hair was crystalline white, cut uncompromisingly short and rising in a cockatoo crest over her innocent maiden forehead.

She was discovered in the large deep garden to be seen at the rear of the house through its wide center hall, down on her hands and knees among the green swords of iris, in a white silk shirt and a many-pocketed canvas skirt.

"Kells! How lovely. Must wipe my dirty hands before extending." She liked him and was pleased to see him, but was suddenly uncomfortable, not knowing exactly what he was doing here. Really, she said to herself, one day I must collect my wits and listen when people tell me things.

When Caroline had announced, with some displeasure, that Kells was coming over she had been thinking hard about her Sarah Bernhardt peonies. Move them to the wall border in back or leave them in the front, where they didn't get *quite* enough sun?

"Will you be staying in the house? I think it's time," with a glance at her watch, "for a glass of sherry. No Caroline to greet you?"

"Roses to Newcastle," Kells said, giving her the box of flowers. "No, I'm at a hotel, I've come to take Markie off for a bit."

He felt the hand tighten in his. Bypassing his good manners, Markie said, "We're not going to sit and *drink*, are we?"

"Briefly," he reassured. Caroline came out into the garden dressed softly in the palest of blue with a faint drift of hyacinth scent about her, a fragrance that for quite a while had annoyed his nose and made him want to sneeze.

No embrace, no kissing, but a light touch of hands. "Let's sit out here and sip, such a lovely day, just like summertime," she said. "And to think that yesterday it was pouring rain and forty-five degrees."

Over sherry, they talked about the weather. The high-walled garden was peaceful, traffic noises dimmed. Anne looked at once welcoming, abstracted and mildly troubled. It could be, Kells thought, that furrow between her brows, what new bulbs to plant now in October; or the Government; or Ian Milford; or a dozen other things. He must manage a private talk with Anne, but had found before that this was like conversing with someone almost unseen in a heavy white mist. Amiable, but just vaguely there.

Caroline was lazily at her ease in her white wrought-iron chair. She had decided on gin and lemon and went at it with the direct immediate thirst of a child. Her hair fell forward to caress her cheeks, her dreamer's face was opalescent ivory in the flickering shadows of the plane trees. Legs crossed, one foot gently swinging, fine fragile instep, airily strapped blue sandal.

Markie sat on the grass beside Kells' chair, giving an occasional visible twitch of impatience. "You'll get your pretty shorts grass-stained," Anne said, looking at him with an expression surprising on her face, eyes intent with love. Kells had always thought her, while well-disposed to those around her, deep in herself and attached to no one.

He tried to put away the sinking, damned-fool feeling. Dashing across the ocean to come to some kind of rescue, and here they all were in a sunny October garden. A set family piece, if a privileged one: idling among borders massed with chrysanthemums, under tree shadow, on a circle of brilliant green silky grass, while the rest of the world went on with its daily work. Markie's inner-lit face showed nothing but happy expectancy.

"Off to meet Ian?" Anne asked Caroline.

"No, he's in Bath. There's a sculpture show I want to see at the Heyward Gallery, Nonny's meeting me."

A further sinking. What if Ian Milford's business in Bath took days, took a week?

"Selling the Crescent, perhaps?" This was put politely by Kells. "I'd hoped to meet him while I was here."

"Oh, a good idea." Caroline sounded as if this thought had just now occurred to her. "We'll see what can be arranged."

Eggshells again. "The zoo, I think," Kells said to Markie as they left the house. "Do you still like the top of the bus?"

He had discarded the idea of a frontal approach. The moment he was alone with Markie, "Now what is this all about?" He thought he could follow, a little, what was going on inside the tow-haired head.

If you don't mention or name a thing or person, it isn't real, it doesn't exist, at least not now. If you are with your own father, have it all, every bit of it. Don't go spoiling things.

And from his viewpoint, maybe with his father here everything might be, yes, who knows, all different and right again.

The direct question, the head-on probing of the trouble—if there was any trouble—might bring on a flood of justification, some of it invented to round things out. Don't demand from him the reasons why he might hate, or fear Ian; or both.

St. James Park didn't feature tigers, nor did the boat running down the Thames to Greenwich and Richmond or up to Kew.

Markie still did like the top of the bus. They walked up Sloane Avenue to the Brompton Road and after a wait climbed onto the bus. On Park Lane, Markie, who had scampered up the stairs and snatched two seats in front, gestured to his right.

"That's where he works." Face momentarily shadowed, turned toward what had once been a lordly town house, pale yellow, balconied, French-windowed and urned on top. The London headquarters of—what was it?—Pruitt and Cream.

Not given to all-out sacrificing of his own comforts for the benefit of the young, Kells conducted Markie firmly past the zoo café, where soft drinks and ice cream were being consumed in quantity, and into the blue-awninged second-floor restaurant, where a seat was found for them by a window. A martini for him, double, while Markie drank lemonade. Roast veal and duchess potatoes and a salad, restoring after the barely touched tray on the plane offering chicken breast congealed in gravy. White wine with it, the usual sip for Markie, who also fancied the froth off the top of glasses of beer.

Drinking his coffee, he reminded himself that this wasn't just any pleasant afternoon, father and son happily reunited because fictitious work had brought him here.

As far as Caroline went, he didn't give a damn whom she married. But there would be the three, not the two of them.

It would mean everything to Markie, or pretty well everything. Nine months of his year, all his years until he grew up and could, if he wanted, go away. My father. My *other* father. The head of the house. *My* house.

They started on what seemed an idle, undirected stroll, Markie content to leave the itinerary in his hands. He was silent now. Sleepy after his lunch, perhaps.

"I suppose you usually have a nap around this time?"

"Sometimes," Markie said evasively.

The Mappen terraces, looking up at the mountain goats, down at the polar bears. The panda was shy today and wasn't to be seen. Passing the gorilla, noble, immemorial, and motionlessly upright on his rump, a woman ahead of them said confidently to her companion, "He's not real, he's a statue, or stuffed, or something," and then gasped as the gorilla swung his head and gazed at her out of his immense quietly blazing eyes.

The lion and tiger installation was new to Kells: open slopes free and green, giving the effect of a country-house lawn. He looked down at Markie and saw his face greenish-colored, pale. Probably just the effect of reflected light from the leaves overhead.

They paused to look at a tiger in a lazy prowl, quite near them. Coin dropped in the slot, voice switched on.

"He said I'd make nice tender tiger food. When we were here. He lifted me up and—"

Calmly, Kells asked, "And what had you done or said before that?"

"I kicked him in the leg."

"Why?"

"I don't remember."

Oh God, Kells thought, here we go again. Markie had probably seen and been infuriated by a joining of hands, or a swift discreet kiss on the nape of a neck. Normal resentful jealous boy aims a kick at the new man when his mother is not looking. Man, rubbing his shin, gets back at him. You might as well learn right now, my boy, that I will not stand for this kind of behavior. You'd make nice tender tiger food—

Unpleasant, vivid, the tearing claws, the blood, the crunch of young bones snapping. But the kicked do not always stop to think.

Arms lifting a thin light struggling body, pretending to be about to hurl him to the nearest beast.

Caroline, at some little distance, turning and seeing them and thinking, Good, they're playing a game together.

Bridget: "He's obviously not used to the company of young children" and "Perhaps there is something of the night about him—"

Markie whispered, looking down at his sandals, "I didn't even tell Bridget. I didn't tell anybody but you." Because, Kells thought, it would be a reenactment, it would be happening all over again—being lifted and swung and about to be tossed to a tiger.

"Lesson number one, Markie, don't kick people, they don't like it. And now, I'm tired if you're not, let's get you back home."

Markie burst into tears and threw his arms around his father's waist. In between the sobs, "Can't I go back to your hotel and stay with you . . . *can't I go back to New York with you . . . ?*"

Racking horrible mistake, to have come at all.

Markie raised his streaked, contorted face to look up into his eyes.

"I belong to you too," he said.

FOUR

Bridget's bedroom overlooked the garden. From above, she finished a fast watercolor sketch of Markie sitting on the grass beside Kells' chair, one fingertip on the top of the mast balancing his sailboat.

The sketch was good; pleasing to one, such as she was, of stern standards. That had been one of the lovely fringe benefits of taking Markie over: drawing, painting, polishing a neglected talent, putting it to hard and steady but adventurous work.

David McEvoy of Fleet Street, the *Daily Mail,* often said, "How *can* you stand it?" And when he had first come to take her out to his three favorite pubs, "Shall I pick you up at the back entrance or do they let you use the front door?"

He didn't have a Della in his past. The dark sour house on grim Corrigan Lane, off O'Connell Street, the grind of sickbed labors, the long entrapment during which you fought resignation and then thankfully collapsed into it. The nothing jobs, ending up with the days, months, years, of designing terrible cheerful greeting cards at Donahue and Sons.

From the beginning, it had been a delightful kind of job. Markie was quiet, of a thoughtful bent, and biddable; they got on well from the first hour. Her manner to him was one of direct simplicity, which he in turn soon adopted.

Not only time to paint, but time to read, and think, and listen to music on her own phonograph, Markie drinking it up. Masses of force-fed fresh air daily, all four seasons of the year; for Caroline, indolent herself, was a great believer in ozone and exercise for the young. Museums and galleries, where Markie, having been introduced to them at the age of three, felt quite at home. Good food, expense no object, prepared in New York by May Ritter, who lived in; and in London by Anne's cook, Mrs. Orme.

All right, David, she would say, it's unambitious and unfashionable and perhaps it's even lazy. I should be clawing my way up in some office, but doing what? How many people do you know who are, day to day, perfectly happy and content with what they do for a living?

There's more to it than that, he would say darkly. There's some magnetic pull that keeps you—at your age, for God's sake, with your brain—a glorified babysitter.

She picked up her watercolor block and did the back of Kells' head, his neck and shoulders and one arm lifted, hand holding his sherry glass, probably to look at the sun striking through it.

How odd to have been snatched for a few seconds by something like nostalgia. To have been thinking, Yes, it has been lovely.

Slight change in the cast on stage, Ian Milford added to it, but was that any reason for the past tense? As far as she could tell he barely noticed her; except for the occasional reading-back glance to extract from her eyes on him the tribute he was probably expecting from any woman.

It wasn't his fault that in some way she could not put her finger on he reminded her of a strange, dangerous man she had known long ago in Dublin. Or that this blurred, fleeting resemblance gave her pause in contemplating him as Markie's future father.

And there was his manner with the child himself; as though, again as actor, he had forgotten his lines and didn't know what to say or how to say it. Now overhearty and now, before he caught himself, annoyed and even peevish. But they'll get used to each other, Bridget told herself without conviction.

She thought it would certainly be to his advantage to learn

how to handle Markie. To put it plainly and simply, a man who married Caroline, her money as well as her beauty, wouldn't have to work for a living if he didn't want to. A proper prize, Caroline was. If you liked that sort of woman, and from the outside looking in Ian obviously did.

How like Kells Markie is, she found herself thinking, looking down into the garden. If Kells was here—of course he was —to meet and take his own measure of the other man, the likeness would become ringingly apparent to Ian. And probably would not further endear the child to him.

It was Kells who paid her salary. That had been the arrangement from the beginning. "It was my idea," he said, "so I will foot the bill." Her bimonthly checks still came from him. How odd the situation would be if for some reason Ian wanted to get rid of faithful, devoted Bridget, Kells' personal woman-on-guard. "He's got to have some kind of continuity. Thank God you provide the better part of that."

Bridget, you will go.

Bridget, you will stay.

And what, David asked, would she do when the time came to send the little darling off to school and she wasn't needed anymore? Look for a job doing ladies' hand laundry?

Markie had private lessons at home now, three days a week, with an out-of-work freshly graduated young Master of Arts from King's College, Cambridge. "He'll have to go to school sooner or later," Caroline said, "but after all the books I've read about those *horrible* good boys' schools and what goes on—"

David's teasing was not meant to be cruel and was not taken as such; his goal was to pry Bridget loose and have her come and live with him. "You wouldn't be very expensive to keep, and the place could certainly use a woman's touch. I can never find my socks and keep having to buy three or four new pairs every week." "Onward and upward," said Bridget. "From mother's-help to custodian of your socks—and unpaid at that."

No, she added, she would not interest herself in ladies' hand laundry. She had her own secret, cherished plan. She would plod boldly from gallery to gallery with a large tape-tied black portfolio under her arm. "I have some things I would like to show you if you have a moment."

Markie would be over but there would still be time, plenty of it. She had just turned thirty in August. For her birthday, Markie had given her a set of spindly, shedding watercolor brushes, tied together with elastic and bought with immense surreptitiousness at Woolworth's, while she on orders kept her back turned. Kells had sent him, to give to her from both of them, a delightful strawberry-pink cape lined in beaver. "He said, my father said, to say it was for park-walking."

Working now at a still life of mauve and russet chrysan-themums gathered this morning, in a battered pewter pitcher, her time flew. At a little after four, she heard two sets of foot-steps in the hall outside, a scurry and a walk.

For reasons she couldn't exactly analyze, she put away her watercolors, her china palette, and her cup of brushes. He was, after all, an artist himself, immensely well paid, up on his professional heights. This delayed her answer to the light knock on the door. "Maybe she's asleep," Markie said outside. "Maybe she's doing my nap for me."

Bridget read a part of the little history of the afternoon in the face, handkerchief-tidied but flushed, the eyes rimmed in red, the long dark lashes in points.

In an everything's-all-right voice which didn't sound like him, Kells said, "Here's your charge back. Hello, Bridget." A hand held out, taking hers in a warm clasp. "I must belatedly report to my office but Markie thinks he can find some time to spare for me tomorrow, I don't know when, right now. I'll call in the morning."

"Lessons until twelve," Bridget said, feeling like a dragon in one of Markie's fairy tales. "Nice to see you, Kells, you're looking well."

"Excuse me, I have to—" Markie fortuitously turned around and raced up the hall to the bathroom.

"Can you come out later," Kells asked swiftly, "and talk to me over something to eat? We didn't get very far on the telephone."

"I'm sorry, I'm afraid I can't. Servants' night out and Caroline's going to a party, I think. Miss Eldredge is apt to fall asleep in the middle of her book, so . . ." She hesitated. "But in any case," and this was hard but necessary to say, "I can't be in the one house—here—and play tale-bearer, or the CIA bringing down a government from inside or underneath."

"I don't ask that. Any facts you might have at hand about this man—not gossip, not random deductions—are all I'm . . ." and then he realized there was no truthful way to finish the sentence. That what he wanted was Bridget's naked uncensored personal reaction to Ian Milford as father-to-be.

He switched directions. "Have you any idea how long Milford is going to be in Bath? No, of course you haven't. Excuse *me* while I disappear as fast as possible."

Going down the stairs, he saw Anne heading for her garden bearing a flat straw basket and shears. He followed her into the open air and feeling like a needle stuck in a record groove said, "I'd like your opinion of Milford, Anne."

Her opinion was just about what he had mentally written for her. "Oh dear . . . I'm not Caroline and men puzzle me, they're so—and most especially *he* is. But people must choose for themselves, mustn't they? They do make frightful mistakes sometimes, but how else would the race—I suppose?—continue itself. And of course the definition of a gentleman has been rewritten and is quite beyond my poor comprehension."

The London branch of Cavanaugh and Cavanaugh was housed in a handsome Portland stone mansion that had once been a gentleman's residence in town, in Allory Place in Mayfair. Perhaps a romantic-seeming and unbusinesslike location, but the agency had made a great deal of money in not doing things the usual or expected way.

"Just ducking in and out, today," he told Miss King.

"Well, we have an office for you so you'll know where to hang your hat if you wore one." She was tall and silver-haired and looked like a marchioness. "Third floor, nice view. Ah, I see the lift knew when you'd arrive, it spends most of its day up on Four."

Large comfortable office, impersonally tidy—who had been abruptly shunted into inferior quarters? Kells had been here only once before, to make a quick tour and meet people and shake hands. A drawing board at right angles to the window and beside it a big bare white-lacquered desk. He sat for a moment at the board gazing at the row of agreeable bal- conied houses across the Place, all of them with gardens on top. Getting up again, he was amused to spot, in the waste- basket, an overlooked scrap of paper with a doodle on it, pursed rosy-red lips, and a number, 68.

An office telephone directory sheet was taped to the side of the desk below the phone. What had that girl's name been? Maisie Something. Here she was on the list, Maisie Tombs, 68. He should, properly, take a walk to her office but he didn't right now want another round of hand-shakings and verbal curtseys. He dialed her number.

"Hello, I'm glad I caught you. Gerald told me to look you up particularly and right away."

"He did?" Short surprised pause. "Well, I *will* be damned. The iron man, sexually speaking." Her voice was high and creamy. "But, on the other hand, what does he think he's run- ning, an advertising agency or a house of ill repute?"

It was after four-thirty. "Can you abandon your labors and come out and have a drink, and if that goes down all right perhaps dinner?" Not his normal way of making contact with strangers; but he was impatient with turning dark corners and finding what seemed to be maddening zeros.

A sigh. "Oh well, droits de seigneur. I did have something else but it was dullish."

"I'll meet you on the steps in five minutes."

"Yes *sir*, and I'd click my heels except I'm in my stocking feet."

She was a short girl of a tough slim build, richly breasted, round-faced, twenty-five or so. Her hair, a shiny and slippery mixture of probably bottled white-gold and dun, was worn like Markie's falling into her eyebrows and petaling her nape. She had the skin of an infant, large and slightly protuberant light blue eyes, and a short straight nose above a mobile full-lipped mouth.

She wore black leather suspendered shorts, a man's white shirt with a black bow tie, and slung over one shoulder a red shirt-jacket that looked remarkably like the uniform of the Canadian Royal Mounted Police. Her black leather boots stopped just below her rounded knees and had tinkling gold bells at the ankles.

He was looked over by her, leisurely, thoroughly, head to foot. "Mmmm, yes—let's see. Not unlike Gerald. *But* unlike him, divorced, or so they say. What bower shall we hie ourselves to, the licensing hours being somewhat in our way? Had you planned to take me to your hotel room? Or that's the way the script was sounding to me."

"Not at the moment," Kells said, liking her immediately. A crazy-like-a-fox girl in her appearance, making her own style and cannily using it, not minding being stared at by passersby but enjoying it. Grist to her professional mill. "Isn't there a private club around here you all have keys to? I believe I was there once with the iron man."

"Yes. Terribly attractive, shame not being able to bag him." She took his arm. "It's just around the corner."

The Private I looked like any other pleasant pub in an expensive part of town, but served nonstop from 8 A.M. to 3 A.M. It was quiet, only a few people at the bar. Maisie led the way to a corner booth for two with tapestry-covered benches. "This is my lucky booth, a special place for seduction."

He picked up their drinks at the bar, a shandygaff for her, a pint of special bitter for himself. After they had touched glasses, Maisie said, "And what—clothed—can I do for you? You obviously don't have to scrounge around the office for a girl to have a drink with."

Relieved at her directness, he went right to the point. "Gerald says you go everywhere and know everybody. Have you ever come across a man named Ian Milford?"

"Ian Milford." She sipped her shandygaff, a drink he had forgotten about, half-and-half ginger ale and beer. "Ian Milford. There's a tag end *somewhere* . . ."

"With a firm called Pruitt and Cream," Kells prompted. "Gilt-edged estate agents. Somewhere in his thirties, handsome I'm told."

"Then why should I connect him with exports?" She took out a monocle and scowled one eyebrow down on it, as though better to observe this distant vision. "Oh, I know. I went to a party at this—yes, import-export man's place in Earl's Court. Six weeks or so ago. There was a girl there, drunk, who kept muttering to anyone within earshot that she'd like to kill Ian Milford. It got to be a kind of party game. People kept coming up to her with suggestions—some quite unusual—about ways to kill Ian Milford. I never knew an overdose by needle of insulin is very hard to spot as a cause of death, I must bear it in mind."

Delivering this last statement, she looked innocent and entirely harmless, a girl well disposed to the world around her. "A dried-up love affair, it seems. Finally she burst into tears and had to be led off to Peter's bed. Peter Queen owns the business. He didn't seem to find any of the killing methods very funny, I gather Milford is an old friend of his."

Having spotted her object, she removed her monocle. "I hope I'm not misleading you. And perhaps this isn't your man at all. It was just a drinking late afternoon, a rotten rainy day, and not the beginning of the crime of the century. She was an actress, I suspect not a good one. Quite pretty. Well, I've dumped and *been* dumped and sometimes it takes you that way."

Kells felt flattened again. For a man to end an affair on the brink of marriage was common prudence.

"Asterisk," Maisie said. "The name of this business place—wholesale and retail shop in front, warehouse behind it—is Queen's Taste. Rather nervy of him sexually, don't you think, that surname?"

With another blank to add to his collection, he set himself out to be pleasant. "If you deal in asterisks, you're a writer, then? I'm afraid I don't know what you do for us."

"Yes, copy. Go Soap, mostly." Go Soap was a product of Streatham Brothers, Britain's mighty rival to Procter & Gamble. Streatham battled Tide with Dazz, Ivory with Flote, and so on right down the line. Cavanaugh and Cavanaugh had thirteen million dollars' worth of Streatham business, which had been the main reason for opening the London office.

"And are you responsible for 'Go Soap yourself'?"

"Who else?"

"Go Soap yourself" had passed into the language on both sides of the Atlantic. The television commercials dealt, lightly and gaily, with doleful or lonely or drab or unsuccessful individuals who, on following the advice to Go Soap themselves, left the screen radiant, wonderful new possibilities obviously waiting for them right outside the shower curtain.

"Actually, your brother, partly," she amended. "It was one of hundreds of ideas we all cranked out and it was sneered upon and buried. Gerald came over in the middle of our first campaign go-round and didn't like the stuff at all and somehow unearthed the thing and pounced on it." She giggled reminiscently. "He said—you know his rumpled scholarly way, peering over his glasses—that it was lewd, crude and rude, therefore exactly right for this year of grace. But I don't want to talk about advertising. I can no longer *bear* not to know why you're so interested in this Milford type."

"He's going to marry my ex-wife," Kells said. "And for nine months of the year he's going to be my son's father."

"Oh, I see. But can't you just look him over and draw your own conclusions? You have rather a knowing eye."

"I can and will I hope, but—" No, don't go into Markie with this affable, sympathetic girl. And right after making this decision, he proceeded to tell her all about it, wanting the objective, dismissing "Perfectly natural, in fact I know a child who reacted the same way in the same situation and then turned out to adore the new man . . ."

Instead, "I can see the problem," she said. "Your living in another country as you do. If things turn sticky, you can't just stroll over to the new ménage and snatch him away to safety."

Safety. Odd strong word for a stranger to use.

With a conscious effort, he cleared his troubled face. "Let's have another drink and flush him for the moment."

"I'll work on him," Maisie promised. "But yes, right now— and it's a good deal more fun to work on *you*—down he goes."

FIVE

A disappointment in a way. Kells Cavanaugh had not, at least immediately, seemed to want his droits de seigneur, his 118 pounds of flesh. But a happy evening, amusing and possibly promising after he had managed to shelve Ian Milford. She was delivered to her door at eleven-thirty and bade farewell with a kind grazing kiss.

Kissing him back soundly, Maisie then yawned and said, "I didn't remember until this moment that when you first called I thought you'd been going to grill me about our office viper."

He looked blank and very tired in the porch light of the carriage house on Farm Street.

"The office manager, Watters, said he'd written to New York about our little trouble?"

"I'd forgotten all about the letter," Kells said. "I'll go to bed and read it. Goodnight, Maisie."

Lying in her own bed, she made her plans for tomorrow morning. Friday was practically the weekend; no serious work was normally undertaken on Allory Place unless a crisis loomed. Perhaps in her next encounter with him she could hand along a gift of information. I am, she thought, a little hooked, I'm charmed practically up to my earlobes. I suppose I have only a few days. We'll see how I rise to the deadline.

Over dinner, shepherd's pie at the Rose and Crown off Piccadilly—("I refuse to stuff ourselves with, say, twenty pounds' worth while people are starving, even though you're on expense account no doubt")—she had said in her forthright way, "There is, I don't know, something about you. Dark and quiet, and what is it? *safe*."

"Father image," Kells said. "Let's have another pint."

The morning was iron gray and cold, a punishment for yesterday's warm sunlight. Well, sermons in stones and good in almost everything, Maisie pointed out to herself: she could wear her new creamy lynx hooded coat, in which she thought she looked like a delicious clutchable bundle.

She took a taxi to the tall pale yellow building on Park Lane. A doorman in matching yellow livery directed her to Pruitt and Cream's offices. Third floor. Elevator to the rear, madam.

She opened a paneled oak door into a little reception room and went over to the desk, where a slim fair woman was talking into the telephone. "Sorry, we do not share listings with other firms, we handle only exclusively. If your present arrangement does not work out, you might choose to come to us."

To Maisie, "Yes, how may I assist you this morning?"

"I have a property I want to place with you," Maisie said, grinned and added, "exclusively. I've been directed by a friend to Mr. Milford."

"He isn't here at the moment, I'll take you to Mrs. Cleat."

"Oh, perhaps I'll come back another time, I did want to see Mr. Milford."

"Mr. Milford is not *all* of Pruitt and Cream," said the woman, perhaps unaware of the warm fond smile that lit her face. "He's in and out and in and out. Mrs. Cleat would be quite irritated with me if I let a property walk out the door."

Oh well, Maisie thought, he might dart in, let us proceed. She followed the receptionist down a carpeted hall, tall white doors opening off it. The first on the right was a little open and she snatched a glimpse. Probably his. Men's-club comfort to it, the gloss of leather, Persian rug, corner of a heavy lion-footed table laden with periodicals, lingering scent of wood fires.

Mrs. Cleat's office defined her relative importance in the firm. Half the size of the clubroom, clean but cluttered, on the other side of the hall, no view of Hyde Park. She was a squat heavy woman in her late forties, with a jowly bulldog face, a thick-lipped mouth drooped at the corners, and untidy dark springy hair. Maisie wasn't to know it, but her reputation in the field was that of a woman savagely, unbeatably successful.

Maisie amended her name slightly; she was, she said, Margaret Graves.

"Do sit down, Ms. Graves, bring us coffee, Dorothy, if you will." Pad and pencil ready.

"Actually the place is my aunt's but she's in New York and asks me to start things moving," Maisie said, and pleasurably continued inventing. "In Cornwall, near the Tamar River. Nine hundred acres, part parkland. The house is a Hawksmoor, wasn't he a pupil of Wren's? Brick, forty-seven rooms, and God knows how many outbuildings, stables and things."

Watching the racing pencil, she stopped to sigh. "I had *so* wanted to see Ian Milford."

Then something happened that caused Maisie to feel as if she had walked in on one of the climactic moments of a play without having seen the explanatory action leading up to it.

Mrs. Cleat cast her pencil on her desk, her face going a curious purple color. She half rose from her chair, then sat down, or collapsed, heavily into it. Her voice upper-register with rage, she said, "I have seen selling major properties for twenty years. Mr. Milford has been with this firm exactly nine months." Pent-up boiling anger, released, seemed to strike the four walls of the room and bounce back from them. God, what a terrifying woman, Maisie thought, feeling the wave battering at her, the elemental force of this woman's emotions.

"I *am* Pruitt and Cream," Mrs. Cleat gasped, "no matter what trimmings we may sport."

Well-versed in the ways of offices, Maisie wondered who had dared place Ian Milford as superstructure on this formidable bastion. Kicking her downstairs—thump, crash. Mrs. Cleat would make quite a crash.

"He won't be here long anyway," the voice sounding directed inward, the bulging dark eyes fiery, "he won't, he won't. She'll tire of him, it's only a matter of time—" And then she stopped herself with a convulsive click in her throat.

She. Who? Kells' ex-wife?

"Sorry," Mrs. Cleat said and, sensible of her, Maisie considered it, didn't try to explain the explosion. "Shall we go on?"

Coffee arrived. "The Long Walk is well-known locally, monkey-puzzle trees on either side of it, a lovely fountain at the foot of the terrace steps, nymphs and dolphins. And a great garden laid out in parterres, mostly roses and yew . . ."

When the description was completed, Mrs. Cleat asked in an exhausted post-rage way, "A snapshot, a photograph would help, have you one or can you get us one?"

After lightning calculation, Maisie said she could probably dig up an old drawing of the house. Have Ben Voight, the art director who had been ousted from his office to make way for Kells, do a sketch, antique it a little. "My aunt did it herself, it's a rather charming view of the house front from the Long Walk. . . ."

If and when Mrs. Cleat discovered this was all a fake, she had visions of a frightful pursuit across Hyde Park, Mrs. Cleat pounding after her with a battle-ax raised and ready.

"I'll have it sent today, Monday at the latest. Or drop by if I'm near." And perhaps get to lay eyes on the mysterious Milford.

But already there was a nice little snippet to pass along to Kells. *She*. She, who was in a position to dump superior officers on Mrs. Cleat's head. She, who would tire of him in a matter of time.

In Maisie's view, women became patrons of handsome men for only two reasons. One, establishing a doting vicarious mother-son relationship. Two, because the men were their lovers.

Did Kells' ex-wife by any wild chance own Pruitt and Cream? He'd have said so, surely.

She stopped at the desk on the way out. "Thank you for the coffee. I am *so* glad I did come here. Now, what was that terribly nice woman's name? I remembered that she had some connection with you. . . . I'd splashed lemonade all over my chiffon at the Queen's garden party and she was so helpful with a batch of tissues—"

"Helpful? Lady Jessica?" Before she could stop herself, the receptionist exhibited surprise.

"Oh yes, Lady Jessica, that's right. Must drop her a note, Lady Jessica . . . mmmm? . . . I'm so awful about names."

"Montroy. But she's in Greece, we don't have a fixed address for her."

"I'll wait until she comes back. When will that be?"

"With Lady Jessica, you never know."

As Markie would be tied up with his Cambridge M.A. all the morning, Kells decided to apply himself to at least a token examination of the trouble at the office, Maisie's viper.

Gerald was constantly at him about attending to important corporate matters. Detesting the business side of business himself, he would cry, "For God's sake, you can't just sit mooning over the drawing board while your own ship is in danger of foundering. I tell you, Kells, you are indolent and have always been indolent. Now then, I haven't time for it, *you* pull yourself together and go talk to Samuelson about the new regulations on pension plans." And he would flee to something not only profitable but far more entertaining.

According to Watters' letter to Gerald, some person in the organization had taken, once a week or so, to leaving insulting, scandalous, or otherwise disturbing messages on the desks of members of the staff; or worse, occasionally pinning them to bulletin boards for passing human traffic to study.

No one had any idea who it was. It could, Watters pointed out doubtfully, be any of the outside people constantly wandering around the agency, free-lance lettering men, photographers and their reps, engravers' men bearing rolls of color proofs to be inspected, models leaving glossies in their wake. To say nothing of delivery boys bearing refreshments at any and all hours. But how would they get to know such, to say the least, intimate details about this person, or that?

"I suppose I could get a detective in here," Watters wrote. "I don't want it to go on, it's bad for morale. People are beginning to look at other people out of the corners of their eyes. But this would be expensive, and our man could be plodding and sniffing around the first floor while lightning is striking silently on the third. What do you advise?"

Kells, a walker by inclination, made his swift way through the dark morning, along Knightsbridge and Piccadilly, struck left on Down Street, which perversely went up, and reached the Portland stone mansion at ten o'clock.

Miss King got up from her desk at the center of the graceful round entrance hall. "I am glad you're here, Mr. Cavanaugh. It's happened again."

From beyond one of the three doors opening off the hall came the sound of muffled weeping. "It's Amy Lauder. There was a note taped to her door and as you can see one has to go past it to get to the elevator *and* the stairs."

She put a distracted hand to her sculptured silver hair. "It said, 'I'd have committed suicide too if I'd been married to you. Happy Anniversary.' It happened, you see, just a year ago today."

Shocked, Kells said helplessly, "Shouldn't she be taken off home? Is there anyone in there with her or is she crying all alone?"

"Yes, Ben Voight, they're quite friends. But she won't go, she says she has a deadline on Bonar's Bread, *Sunday Times Magazine.*"

"I think," Kells said, "if you can find a radio somewhere you'd better bring it out here and fill the air with music. She's a commercial all by herself, poor girl, for the Trouble at

Cavanaugh and Cavanaugh. And I suppose I'd better talk to Watters right away."

Business seemed, however, to be much as usual as he ran up the stairs. Through open or half-open doors, voices, laughter, the tapping of a typewriter, a man talking forcibly to his dictating machine: ". . . our meeting was in every way a success. They have decided to go with the Sexy Sesame Bread, I think we can get away with it. I told them the commercials—casting, voices, music, sets—would absolutely *steam* sex. I don't believe any other bakery has ever mined this particular lode . . ."

No, not quite as usual. From the far end of the corridor on the second floor, a girl's voice, high, edged with hysteria. "I could understand blackmail, there's some point in that. Shouldn't they get the police in, shouldn't they take fingerprints off these filthy notes and then fingerprint everybody here?"

A man answering, laughing, not a nice laugh. "Hardly a police matter. But *you've* nothing to be afraid of, darling. Or have you?"

Watters was waiting in Kells' office. He was a small pale damp-looking man with little dark mole eyes that were given to blinking as though the daylight after his tunnel was too much to face. Extremely efficient, though. "You should hear him haggling over the price of two new electric typewriters," Gerald said.

"This note this morning, same style," Watters reported. "Page torn off a five-by-seven-inch scratch pad, everybody uses them. Art people, copy people, everybody. Block printing, not bad but not skilled—although an art director might have to forget his training to do it that way. The office opens at nine, King's back is to Mrs. Lauder's door, people streaming by and running around, only thing on their minds to get to their offices in a hurry and settle down to a hearty lingering breakfast—"

What if it were you? Kells thought idly, and then saw how

the petty office nonsense as it was seen by Gerald could seep softly, poisonously, through the air.

"And you've no idea at all, no slightest suspicion?"

"None. Can't very well call a meeting of the whole agency and ask whoever's responsible to raise his hand. My idea was that the less open attention paid to it the better. If you drop a pebble in a pool and there aren't any ripple rings, you might lose interest."

Sound enough; except that the weeping downstairs might have provided a very satisfactory ripple for the perpetrator. Casual, random sadism was not one of the more attractive vices.

"Someone with a chip? Who, say, expected a raise or a promotion and didn't get it?"

"As I see it," Watters said severely, with a series of blinks, "everybody here is already overpaid. But that's yours and your brother's affair."

He tried to thrust away his second sweep of suspicion. (The complaining snarl just underneath the surface of the voice.)

"Are there any obvious eccentrics around?"

"They are *all* eccentrics to me," said Watters, who had been born and raised in grimy Deptford, in a small semi-detached brick house unpleasantly close to the Foreign Cattle Market.

"Well," began Kells. Well what? He had a wild desire to say, "Carry on, Watters!" in the distantly receding voice of empire.

"Well, there are what, thirty or so people here, sooner or later our man will run out of material."

"Or woman," Watters said. "I always connect this kind of thing with women. If you have no immediate suggestions—I mean *other* suggestions, Mr. Cavanaugh—I must get back to my work."

Kells soon found that he had joined the club. The In box on the desk was piled with papers. His name had been hastily written in on seven interoffice memos, which he put aside for later-if-ever reading. There was an invitation to a cocktail party on Half Moon Street from someone named Elizabeth Mayne. And at the bottom, a five-by-seven-inch sheet of scratch pad paper.

It said: "Well, what do you expect, when a child of divorce is thrown to the four winds?"

After a few stunned seconds, intellect came to the aid of the shot-in-the-stomach feeling.

It wasn't a threat, the note, and it exhibited no extrasensory perception. It was a perfectly ordinary good guess about divorce, about a child, about the normal emotions involved, especially when the child was in one country and the father lived in another. His marital affairs were probably common knowledge here as well as in New York; even non-gossips liked to get people straight, with emphasis on the people who paid their salaries. Not married? Why? Is he queer? Oh, he was married, up until two years ago, there's a son, mostly with the mother.

Not a threat, just a nose impudently tweaked. A sore foot deliberately stamped on.

Nevertheless, he put the note in his billfold. Keep it quiet, don't sent it echoing around the agency. The less open attention paid to it, the better. It would be a little like stripping himself naked for a trip down the wide, curving, carpeted stairway.

How many other people kept, in pain, these communications quiet?

But, to hell with Cambridge, reading, writing, and arithmetic. He ought at least to say good morning to Markie.

A man's voice answered. English, educated, rich in timbre. "We're in a bit of a bother here, although we think probably he's gone running to you. He's been, for about eight minutes, a missing person."

SIX

"Bridget around?"

"No, I've sent her off to Marks & Spencer's for cashmere sweaters for Markie—they're on sale. Why?"

"I've been thinking it might be a good idea to end the Bridget phase."

What did that mean? Nothing good. It translated simply into "end Bridget." Never a devious child, Markie had been forced by events into an intense, listening awareness.

He had come downstairs to get his sailboat, which he had left last night in the library. The two of them—his mother, whom he loved, had become not *her* or *she* but *they* and *them*—were having breakfast in the small yellow room overlooking the garden. A cup clinked against a saucer. A parrot in a cage in one of the windows harshly sang a calypso line, "Hey, Mister Tallyman, tally me banana," and then added hollowly, "Markie, Markie!"

He was hidden from their view by the angle of the folding door but he moved closer against the wall.

"Oh but, Ian, she's an institution. And where on earth would you ever find someone so dependable and so, I don't know, exactly right? And again, why?"

"I don't think she likes me, and oddly enough I like to be liked in my own household. It makes me suspect her loyalties may lie with Kells. After all, he's male, she's female. There may be tale-bearing, friction, when she goes off to him in New York—I mean, darling, why drag bits and pieces of your past into our delightful present?"

Markie felt a faint trembling somewhere far inside his rib cage.

"Given you something to think about, haven't I? And, far more important, I think he depends too much on her and is too attached to her. With something so fresh and new and fine starting . . ." A pause. Was he taking her hand, or kissing her? ". . . we don't want the cobwebs and the spiders, do we? From now on, his first and strongest dependence should be on *us*."

Us. Us. Them.

"Surely you do see that, Caroline? I *want* to be Markie's father, his check and balance, his port in a storm. We've all three of us, I hope, a long and happy life ahead."

"Well . . ." She sounded as she always did when someone was trying to force her into something she didn't want to do. "Give me some time to think about it. You've shaken me up."

"All right, no wild hurry. But my idea would be a competent woman, a different one every year so peculiar affections don't build up. And in any case he won't be needing a nursemaid or companion or whatever Bridget is much longer." Sound of a silver dish cover being removed. "More bacon? By the way, speaking of Marks & Spencer's, don't you think it's time the baby name was dropped? Let's begin on, simply, Mark."

Markie wanted to shout his rage and fear, and kick at the door shielding him. Instead, he slipped out from behind it and up the stairs, having forgotten all about his sailboat. He heard behind him the front door opening, the maid's polite greeting.

"Hello, Rose," said Roderick Wyse. Her name was Rosamund but Anne said that was a bit dressy and firmly decreed the short form.

Wyse went laboriously, his head throbbing, up the stairs to the front sitting room, where he proposed, somehow or other, to instruct Markie this morning. He had been at a party in Soho until four in the morning, at least he thought it was four, the latter end of the party had vanished.

Markie looked up into the large-nosed, blue-eyed, golden-bearded face. In his charming husky warble, he said, "You've been given the morning off, because of my father. He's here from New York."

On a brisker morning Wyse might have wondered, and checked this with the authorities. But his relief knew no bounds. He could go back and get into the bed he hadn't wanted to get out of. Anyway, he had had no trouble with tricks or games or insubordination so far; Markie was a thirsty and absorbed learner.

"Don't make a noise going out," cautioned Markie. "My aunt has an awful headache and is trying to sleep late."

They, in the yellow room, would be too busy with their breakfast and each other to see Mr. Wyse silently leaving the house.

His private but legal store of money, about two pounds in coins and a one-pound bill, was kept in an old and still scented cinnamon tin in his bedroom. Hurry, before Bridget got back—Bridget, who must be saved. He was strictly forbidden the streets outside the court by himself, but this was different. Misled by the memory of yesterday's sun, he put on a Shetland pullover. The rest of him was dressed, gray flannel shorts, blue shirt, blue socks, and crepe-soled brown shoes, good for tiptoeing.

Emerging at the foot of the back stairway, he crossed the freshly scrubbed kitchen floor. "Where are you going, young Markie?" Mrs. Orme, the cook, asked.

"Out to get my sailboat."

"Oh, he's giving you lessons in yachtsmanship this morning, is he?" But she was busy with her scones, and there was the shopping to be done, hurry with the scones before the rain comes on; and she forgot to observe that his was a one-way passage across her clean floor.

In the garden, the yellow room windows were to his left. He turned right and went under the arbor at the side of the house which in summer was fragrantly burdened with white roses. The mossy paving stones of the path smelled damp and green, smelled of escape and victory.

He wouldn't let them do it. Not his father.

The cold wind hit him as he ran down the narrow sidewalk between the parked cars and the painted gay house fronts. The street, Sloane Avenue, so much warned against, looked quiet, very few cars. Get off the corner and out of sight of the house. There were no empty cabs to be seen. He ran up the street, looking back over his shoulder for possible pursuers. This resulted in his tripping on a slightly uneven paving stone and falling hard, landing on one knee and skinning it painfully.

The next street over, Draycott Avenue, looked busier and more promising. He turned the corner at narrow Ives Street, reached Draycott, and saw a taxi with its vacant light on and signaled it with both arms waving. It drew to the curb beside him, just in front of a vegetable barrow. From behind dashed a woman carrying an immense brown paper bag with a loaf of French bread sticking out at the top.

"Thank you, little boy!" she shrieked. "Aren't you kind!" She firmly took Markie's hand off the door handle, grasped it herself and jumped in. As if on cue with this act of piracy, the rain started.

An unseen Bridget at his side said, "Oh lord, now we'll never get a cab, not in this rain, we'd better take cover and wait for a bus." But he didn't know how to get to Allory Place by bus.

"I think he depends too much on her. . . ." Spiders and cobwebs. Bridget? Bridget, who smelled of wet grass, and fresh lavender in the sun?

In unconscious obedience to her, he took shelter under an awning in front of a butcher's shop on Brompton Road. All the traffic seemed to be coming in the other direction, on the opposite side. After hesitating, he crossed carefully with the lights but was frightened by the cars turning swiftly, the light theirs too, out of Pelham Street into Brompton.

". . . don't you think it's time the baby name was dropped?" But if he wasn't to be Markie anymore, who was he? If they called him by another name, would he be some-one else? For a second or two he had a dizzying, slipping-away sensation.

Here at last was another cab, empty. The driver, at the curb, turned and gave his would-be passenger a long stare. "Nineteen Allory Place," Markie said, his voice something of a croak with breathlessness, chill, and worry.

"You got any money?" the driver inquired.

"Three pounds," Markie said. "Right in my pocket." He got it out. "Look. There's this bill and—"

"All right then, Christopher Robin."

He didn't put the meter flag down and Markie wondered about that but was afraid to say anything for fear of being put out on the street. However, they were moving, they were on their way to Allory Place. Soon he found his bearings, Knightsbridge, St. George's Hospital, where sometimes he and Bridget boarded coaches for Kew Gardens or Greenwich. Pic-cadilly now, the Duke of Wellington astride his horse Copen-hagen, Green Park to the right, then the Ritz, where his mother had taken him to tea for his birthday. The Ritz door-man was blowing his whistle and waving his arm. Under the canopy stood a man and woman with a pile of luggage beside them.

"Good-oh, Heathrow," said the driver as if to himself, and pulled over. "That'll be three pounds even, including the tip, mate."

"But this isn't . . ." The door was pulled open, the door-man's hand helped him vigorously out. "Oh, thank God," said the woman, "I thought we'd *never*—"

"Cross right up there at the lights," the driver called to Markie. "Go back down a couple of blocks to your left, and then up Down Street." And rapidly pulled away.

Markie made a discovery. Being cheated felt like a hard un-expected slap over the face and produced the same startled effect, a sting of tears in the eyes. The doorman, who in his uniform looked very much an authority figure, might demand to know who he was and somehow send him home. So he followed what he thought might be unreliable directions but better than none at all and crossed Piccadilly.

His vision momentarily blurred, he stumbled on one of the metal studs edging the crossing and almost fell. Traffic, told by the signal to advance, sprang as if there were no one in its path at all. He made it to the curb by a tenth of a second, landing on his hands.

The rain was coming down hard now, bouncing back up six inches from the sidewalk. Soaked and beginning to shiver, he walked slowly down the slope. Back and to your left? But to his left was the park, across the street.

A woman carrying an umbrella, and with a dachshund on a leash, stopped beside him. Her voice was kind. "You look lost to me, are you? Where are you going, all alone in the rain? And your poor *knee*."

The tears, which hadn't quite stopped, wanted to begin again. "Allory Place," Markie said hoarsely. "Nineteen. My father."

"Come, get under my umbrella and I'll escort you almost there, my house is just a block away."

What with the coming and going of taxis at number nineteen, Cavanaugh and Cavanaugh's Allory Place neighbors found the agency the next best thing to a hack stand.

Kells, watching tensely at a window in the entrance hall, saw Maisie arrive and make a dash for the door, clutching her furs close against the wind and rain.

Inside, she said, "Oh, *you*, how nice! Am I in time to reserve you for lunch? I have news to impart."

"I don't know . . . I'm afraid not," Kells said, sounding vague to her, strange, not somehow there at all.

He kept telling himself not to worry. Under the circumstances, Markie might be tempted to run away from home. But he would never run away from Bridget. Would he?

He would appear any minute now. Wouldn't he?

"I wish, excuse the rhyme, that Kells was in hell," Ian Milford said. "Christ, what a bore, having him turn up just now. Stop worrying, Caroline, of course he's gone running to him."

Anne had left the house ten minutes ago to search nearby for Markie. "Can't you just hear her?" Ian said. Then, his voice going up and sounding so like Anne's that Caroline almost laughed in spite of herself, "*Have* you by any chance seen my great-nevoo? *Is* he in your garden or playing with one of the—mmmm— You do have children or at least the people in the pink house do, or is it the green?"

Anne, coming in the back way, heard him. A quiet burning dislike and distrust, not new, gathered force in her. She stayed where she was, just inside the kitchen door.

Ian reached for his trench coat, which he had flung in an ownerly fashion on the drawing-room sofa.

"You're not going to leave me here chewing my nails?" Caroline asked. "And shouldn't we call the police just in case?"

"Not unless he fails to surface at daddy's place of business. And yes, I am going to leave you. He has to be fetched back. He's for the time being in your custody, not his father's. We have to start somewhere, don't we, and why not right now?"

He didn't add that it would look odd, their just sitting on their hands assuming the child was safe. A worried parent-to-be must, flawlessly, act like one.

Bridget, not fond of shopping at best, was a little wearied after the battle of the cashmere sweaters, in which she competed with and was elbowed and trampled by a social gamut running from country gentry to Pakistanis.

She had finally managed, reaching over the shoulder of an

enormous fat woman, to pick up off the untidied stacks three
sweaters in the right size, cherry red, yellow, and brown.

After paying for them, she came to a stop beside the boys'
coatrack. Markie needed one, he'd outgrown last year's, and
rather than face another trip here in the immediate future,
she took a quick look through. This one, just the thing, a very
nice camel's-hair polo coat, warmly lined in wool plaid. Forty
pounds. High, but although Caroline was a devoted follower
of sales—when she didn't have to attend them herself—and
somewhat of a penny counter on occasion, she liked Markie to
look well-turned-out.

Wise to call first, though. Bridget went to a rank of wall
phones and dialed the house. Rose answered. "Oh, Bridget,
something awful. Markie's gone, lost, or rather they think he
may have gone to Mr. Cavanaugh, but everybody's all upset—"

"I'd better go and see if he has," Bridget said.

Miss King, busy at her desk, was nevertheless puzzled by
the taut waiting silhouette at the arched floor-length window.

Expecting his son, he had said. How motionless he was. He
made her uncomfortable. "Shall I have someone bring you
coffee, Mr. Cavanaugh? Or perhaps"—it was close on eleven
o'clock—"a glass of sherry?"

"Thanks, no." He leaned forward as another cab drew up. A
man in a trench coat got out, looked up and down the street,
and then turned to pay the driver through the window. He
was tall and strikingly handsome, looking to be in his mid-
thirties. He had longish silver-gold hair, superbly cut and arranged in lion locks, pale silver eyes rimmed with thick dark
lashes, a long chin that came to a point, a fine nose, and an
oddly secret and sensual mouth. From the sidewalk, through
glass and stone, he projected stage presence.

Kells found himself registering every detail and wondered
why, although his subconscious immediately knew why.

Turning toward the steps, the man stopped. Markie—*thank
Christ, Markie*—must have rounded a near corner and was

now, running, in view. The man in the trench coat swooped. To the sound of a shriek, Kells flung the front door open.

It couldn't be, it couldn't be, not after he'd come all this way. Ian Milford seemed to him unreal, a figure of nightmare, bending, holding out his arms, a great barrier blocking his path to his father.

"I hope you're satisfied, Markie, you gave us one hell of a scare."

Another wild cry, half muffled against the breast of the trench coat.

"For God's sake let him go," a voice ordered from the top of the stairs.

SEVEN

Ian straightened and Markie dashed to his father.

"I suppose we'd better take ourselves in out of the rain to settle this? I suppose also you're Kells Cavanaugh?"

Kells held the door open. "Settle what? Come in."

Miss King, at her desk, shot to her feet at the sight of the wet, bloody-kneed little boy. "Oh, poor dear, and shivering too, shall I take him along back and tidy up the scrape?"

"No, I'd better," Kells said. "You might see to Mr. Milford."

Around the waist of the hall, which lifted two stories, was a wrought iron-railed circular corridor from which what had once been bedrooms and were now offices opened. Spectators appeared. Miss King had a carrying voice and Kells' was raised too, in buoyant relief.

"Honestly," Liz Mayne said a little later, "the two of them! The Montagues and the Capulets if I ever— That rather fascinating silver-and-gold man and the dark one—Kells, isn't it? —facing each other, *so* formal and polite."

"You aren't proposing to hijack Markie?" Ian Milford asked. Outrageous suggestion, delivered in a mildly amused voice.

"No. Dry him off and clean his knee. You might call Caroline."

The large original main floor powder room near the rear of the house had been divided into Ladies and Gentlemen. Each was equipped with a well-stocked medicine cabinet. While Kells gently blotted blood with warm water and gauze pads, Markie poured out his tale, badly interrupting himself with hiccups.

They were going to end Bridget, send her away. They

couldn't do that, they couldn't, could they? And the woman who had stolen his taxi, and then being let off at the Ritz and all his money gone. And he wasn't to have his own name anymore, or any peculiar affections.

The bandaging finished, Kells applied himself to stopping the hiccups with a glass of water. "One thing at a time," he said. "No, they will not send Bridget away, at least not for quite a while, calm down. Sip from the wrong side of the glass. Where was she, to let you run out of the house like that? Here's a cloth, you might give your face a wash."

"Shopping for sweaters for me," Markie said from the depths of the dripping cloth. "But everything will be all right now?"

"As all right as I'm able to make it." Which could be read, Kells thought grimly, several ways. He ought to have guessed that Milford might plan to start out with a new crew aboard his boat, not the ex-captain's possibly rebellious remnants.

"And you won't let him take me back?"

"Of course you have to go back, it's where you happen to live, Markie, but not until you're okay again." He peeled off the damp sweater.

A clash in the entrance hall wouldn't do. He took Markie upstairs to the third-floor office in the lift, established him in a chair by the radiator, and called the desk. "Will you send Mr. Milford up, Miss King?"

Entering the office, Ian said, "Well, all ready, Mark? I called your mother and she's of course frantic." He had taken off his coat to reveal splendid easy tailoring which seemed not to have been informed of rain and wrinkles, right down to his glossy shoes.

"I won't go with him," Markie said, head turned away. "I won't."

A battle of wills wasn't indicated, not here, not now, not in front of him.

Forcing a quiet pleasant tone, Kells said, "We'll give him time to warm up and then I'll bring him along."

"No, sorry. I insist. All right, ten minutes, although cabs are sheltered places. I am, Cavanaugh, quite a nice chap and I refuse to accept for a moment the role of Mr. Monster. Mark and I are good friends and will soon be better ones."

Markie, looking out the window, said, "*I hate you.*"

There was a shock of silence. Ian's face went scarlet and his silver eyes narrowed. The color might have been rage or humiliation or both. Kells found himself briefly sorry for him. This wasn't the petulant whine of a foot-stamping child balked in some favorite object by a maddening grown-up; but chillingly measured, direct, and meant.

From his breast pocket, Ian took out a slim black morocco cigarette case and looked at its contents as though he had forgotten what his hand next intended to do.

At the light knock at the door, he turned to open it. Bridget came in, Bridget in her raincoat with her umbrella. She looked at the two men's faces and then went over to Markie. "I've come to take you home, scarperer. I have a cab waiting, we must hurry up. Hello Kells, hello Ian."

There was a clear indication that they two might have business of their own; but that Markie was her business.

He turned wordlessly and put his hand in hers. He gave Kells a single glance, forlorn and defeated, that pierced him. The pair left the room, Bridget saying, "I don't need my sweater, not under this coat, you shall have it when we get in the cab and no one will see how funny you look in it."

"Solution number three," Kells said as Ian shrugged one arm into his trench coat. "Proving again, what would we all do without Bridget?"

Maisie kept an eye on the odd little crisis which had shown signs of starting in the hall, in between dabbling at the new series for "Go Soap Yourself." She wouldn't start serious work on the commercials until Monday, too many things on her mind.

Ben Voight jibbed a little at doing her country-house drawing, which she wanted right away. She had given him a typed description of the imaginary residence. "For God's sake,

Maisie, I'm up to here in work and there's Amy to comfort, she keeps breaking down in the middle of paragraphs about her bread, poor lamb. Every time I give her a brandy I have one with her and already I'm half crocked."

"I can't tell you why right now, but this is important, in a way agency business."

She saw Ian Milford go back to the lift and disappear. Then through her wide-open door she heard Miss King say, "They're up in Mr. Cavanaugh's office, yes, the little boy too."

Going to the rail, she looked down at the woman standing in front of the desk. Strong and fresh, solidly slender. Skin of taut cream and roses, dark brows and lashes and dark bare head. Maisie thought she had a kind of solemn, steady beauty and got what she later identified as a sinking feeling, she had no idea why.

Could this be Caroline Cavanaugh?

"If the driver gets impatient and comes in here looking for me, will you tell him to wait, it's important?"

"Yes indeed, Miss Dorsey," said Miss King.

Three minutes later, the Dorsey woman and Kells' little boy going out at the front door. Followed in another two minutes by Ian Milford.

Maisie went back to her office and tried for the third time to reach her sister-in-law Hildegarde. The line had been engaged for half an hour. This time she got her.

"I just had a memory tickle and I thought you could help. Wasn't it your brother or was it his cousin who was mixed up at one time with Jessica Montroy?"

"Oh God, yes," Hildegarde said. "Practically torn to pieces, poor boy, of course he was much too young to take her on."

"What was she like, did you ever meet her?"

"Once. A sort of contemporary Nancy Cunard. Swallows men as restoratives. Very handsome. Raunchy, tough I've heard— Money unlimited. He, Montroy, owns about a fourth of the best part of London, lets her have things pretty well as she wants them. He goes to his club and plays billiards when he isn't gentleman-farming. I'd say she was somewhere in her late thirties. What was it someone said about Byron? 'Mad, bad, and dangerous to know.' Well, I see her as a bit like that. But I suppose I'm prejudiced. Robbie did try to kill himself, even if he didn't try very hard."

It was now close on twelve o'clock. She dialed Ben Voight's number and Kells answered.

"Are you back on earth now, from that other planet you were occupying a little while ago?"

"Yes. Markie had gone missing but as you may have heard he turned up here."

"Not to repeat myself, but will you take me to lunch at one? I've spent part of my morning at Pruitt and Cream." Kells said yes, he would.

"I may come in disguise, a Hallowe'en mask or something. By now a woman named Mrs. Cleat may have looked up country properties in Cornwall and may be headed this way with a loaded gun." On this mysterious note she hung up.

He was glad she'd nailed him because right on the heels of her call he got three other invitations to lunch. From Axel, the head of the creative department; Wilkinson, the account man on Bonar's Bread; and the money man, Cowles. A little guilt-ily—suppose there was important business to go into, and not just exchanges of courtesies with the visiting fireman?—he said no, thanks very much.

As soon as the dust cleared after Markie's return to Anne's house, he would have to call Caroline about Bridget; and tell her that if she was considering firing her, to forget it.

And if she said no, Bridget goes?

While he was turning these things over in his mind, he was outwardly being intent on the problems of Perce's Cat-Manna catfood, which the account man, Entwhistle, had brought to his office to lay before him.

"They've been canned, solids, so far, but they think of going to kibble. However, that would mean new equipment, an extension to the plant, and . . ."

At this earth-trembling time of Markie's life, he must have Bridget. "If you continue to insist, Caroline—or rather if Milford does—I must take up my option of having him with me for six months, not three." Who would take care of Markie while he was off at work and often away from home for a week? Where was there another Bridget?

". . . and the new Beef Casserole Mix isn't going well, they want advice from us as to whether to take it off the line. I have some sales figures here, past and projected, I'd like you to look at and then I'd like to have your thinking on it."

Oh God, he'd forgotten, or hadn't had the time, to warn Markie not to pass along his information about her to Bridget. She might fly into a well-justified rage. You can't fire me, I quit. She might pack her bags and go. Today.

"I can see," Entwhistle said, "that I've really got you thinking. We must coddle them particularly right now, they're thinking of going into dogfood and they could very well give *that* chunk to another agency if we don't show that we're in there fighting for them every inch of the way."

"You might say clawing for them," Kells said.

"Yes. Ho." He laughed a little. "Good, yes, clawing. But to get back to the dogfood, I wouldn't be surprised if their advertising budget was double what they put out for the catfood . . ."

Governments rise and bloodily fall, war plans are being laid, even for the ultimate one, great events roar onto the pages of history, Kells thought, while all the time people all over the world sit in conference and talk—indefatigably—about plant extensions and budgets and projected sales figures.

He gave an open and extended glance at his watch.

"Oh, sorry, you probably have a thousand things to— I'll just leave this comprehensive folder for your later study. Perhaps we can get together before day's end." The folder must hold seventy or so sheets of paper.

"Glad to, if I'm here." He'd just ask Maisie, Kells decided. She could probably tell him all about Cat-Manna in seven sentences instead of seventy pages.

He called Caroline. Immediately, she said, "Really, Kells, I think you should make every effort to put a stop to this kind of thing, he's never been this naughty before, you are absolutely *ruining* discipline, to say nothing of— He could have been run over and killed, he could have been kidnapped—"

"I haven't time to talk, or rather to listen, I'll see you later. In the meantime, I'll have your head, Caroline, if you rock the ship. About Bridget, I mean. That's what sent him running."

"You have no power over me, legal or otherwise," Caroline said in soft fury. "Except through Markie, and you wouldn't want to *use* him, would you?"

"No. Would you?"

From the doorway, Maisie said, "Here I am, wrapped, ribboned, and ready."

It wasn't she who terminated the call. Caroline had just hung up.

"I'd thought about asking you to come home with me because I have to feed the cat," Maisie said as they stepped into a taxi at the steps which a man with a huge brown envelope had gotten out of. "But, for you not for me today seemed not quite the mood for it. Perhaps tomorrow, and that will give me time to go out and buy a cat."

She had suggested that they go to a pub that had been her second home when she worked on Park Lane, the Swallow. "It's right around the corner from Pruitt and Cream and you never know. He is somewhat of a dazzler, isn't he? Although on the whole not a man I'm sure I'd trust with my tender . . . heart."

Kells gave her a look of amused affection. "You're just being loyal, Maisie."

She took off her glove and put her hand in his. "Just tell me when you're getting too excited and I'll let go at once."

"I'm afraid," suddenly leaning forward to look to his right, "it has to be at once. Stop a minute, driver, will you?"

A telephone call was tricky: too many ears. He went into the small florist's shop and from the glass case chose white roses, most of them in bud. He asked the girl in the pink smock for a card. His urgent worries ran away with his hand, or so he put it to himself later.

"Please dear darling indispensable Bridget, don't move a muscle until I can talk to you, Kells."

He asked that the flowers be delivered right away and the girl said yes, right away, the messenger was playing solitaire in the back room.

"As they obviously weren't to me," Maisie said when he rejoined her, "let me think who my rival is. I'll give myself one guess. That dark girl, the one who marched in and smartly removed the son and heir. But that isn't fair odds for me—you his father and she seeming for all the world like his mother—"

She was relieved to see his look of blank astonishment.

"Your *rival—!*"

"Oh well, that's all right then. Here's my hand again."

At the Swallow, she said, "Let's sit at the bar, you can pick up all sorts of things at bars. Hello, Joyce," to the tall rosy dark-haired woman behind the bar, "it's been ages."

"First one's on the house, Maisie love, for you and your chum," said Joyce. After pleasantries she moved down the crowded bar and Maisie announced, thirstily lifting her half pint of lager, "Now I will tell all."

She made short but pithy work of it and was not interrupted by so much as a syllable from Kells. How dear he looks, she thought, his eyes getting bigger, like a kid's.

In conclusion, she remarked blandly, "Of course it may all be perfectly innocent. But it does look a bit odd, doesn't it? Almost like a kept man, except in a respectable office instead of lying around in a boudoir eating chocolates, that wouldn't do for a man, would it. Nice job—and he certainly has the looks and style for stalking about immense castles and things —and no doubt a very nice salary. I wonder if Caroline will mind about her?"

There was motion directly behind them. A hand fell on Maisie's shoulder and another on Kells'. "Marcie!" cried the man, kissing her on the back of the neck.

"Maisie," she said, turning. "Hello, Peter. Kells Cavanaugh, Peter Queen."

Peter Queen looked to be mildly, merrily drunk. He was a tall man with a thin triangular fey face, Dutch-cut shiny brown hair with the bangs falling into his small, brilliant blue eyes. His nose was aristocratically hooked; his mouth had lifted elfin corners as though he was secretly amused about something no one else knew. He wore an expensive smoke-green corduroy suit with a Burberry tossed over one shoulder.

"I'd thought Ian might be here to help me celebrate," he said. "You two come and help instead. I've snaggled a corner over there big enough for three. First I have to go to the loo, won't be a tick."

"Must we?" Kells asked after he had moved away. He wanted to go on talking to Maisie, whose analysis of Milford's daily work might be quite mad, or wholly correct.

Maisie said, "You came all the way over the ocean, my sweet Kells, not to send flowers to your Irishwoman or buy me lager and help me feed the cat—but to see what Ian Milford is all about. Of course we will join his oldest friend, also, I believe, from Rhodesia."

With fresh drinks in hand, they picked their way through a babble of lunchers, sitting and standing, eating and drinking, to the far corner to which Peter Queen had laid claim with an umbrella straddling the angle of the red leather bench. When he rejoined them, carrying a pint in each hand—("All for me, chaps, save me a trip")—Maisie asked what they were celebrating.

"I've just sold a great old bed for pots and pots." He beamed into the first of his pints. "And *pots.*"

"I didn't know you dealt in furniture," Maisie said with polite uninterest.

Sounding unaccountably cautious and deflated, Queen amended, "Well, you know, the odd bits and things one stumbles upon in Taiwan—not a bed actually but a bed*head* of wicker, elaborate, very lacy, quite charming . . ."

He put his glass mug down with a thump. "I drank my way

up here, I think I ought to have something to eat, next thing I'll—" The merriment vanished before their eyes; he seemed to withdraw into himself.

"I saw someone at the bar eating a smoked salmon sandwich," Maisie said. "Let's all have some. By the way, Peter, in case the name hasn't registered, Kells used to be married to Caroline."

"And who," Queen asked, "is Caroline?"

The level of the noise in the pub remained undimmed but in their corner a humming silence took over for a moment.

Maisie told Kells later that she knew she'd dropped a clanger and had no idea of the whys and hows; and that she thought from there on in it was his personal business, not hers, she was after all only an interested bystander. "Some people, men as well as women, do keep their lives in compartments. I had no right to push over Milford's dominoes for him."

Now she said, "My turn for the loo," and stepped over Kells' legs.

In the flick of a second, Kells remembered, from Caroline's letter to him in New York, ". . . it's all rather a secret, so don't tell everybody." Did everybody include Milford's oldest friend?

He saw no reason to join the pair in deviousness.

"Caroline and Milford are going to be married before the end of the month," he said. "Or perhaps you know her by some nickname?"

"I don't know her at all," Queen said slowly. "You're not making this up? No— Excuse me while I fetch myself a plate of something."

He took his umbrella with him to get a plate of something.

He did not reappear.

EIGHT

Caroline was all soft motherhood when Markie came in at the front door and was handed over by Bridget.

Down on one knee to him, arms out, no scolding except a gentle, "My darling lamb," tears in her eyes, "you did give us a fright but now you're all safe and sound." The arms holding him, warm, the flowery scent of her, the kiss on his damp tumbled hair.

Seizing the advantage, he said, "Then you won't, you won't—"

"Won't what, Markie?"

Bridget had paused halfway up the stairs and was watching them. "What he's asking," she said firmly, "is that you will not carry through the plan to send me packing."

Markie had told her everything in the taxi, raggedly but at least three times over and making himself perfectly clear.

Caroline got up gracefully and looked hard at Bridget. "Who's been eavesdropping? But of course you were out shopping. . . ."

"He wasn't eavesdropping, he was looking for his boat." But why am I defending him? Bridget thought. It's finished, it's over. I think.

A normal rage had swept her, in the cab. She had said bitterly to herself in the classic fashion, After all I've done for this child—and then, inside, she had laughed bitterly, too. What had she done, looking at it squarely, but settled and sunk into a lovely job that couldn't have suited her better? And had the time of her life for three years. Take the goods the gods provide, and don't stand and sulk when they are snatched away from you.

The old, venomous Irish tag ends floated through her mind. *I know where I'm not wanted . . .* and, *the back of my hand to you.* The pathetic spittings of the rejected. Be quiet about it, hold your spine straight.

Anne came into the hall from the drawing room, where she had been tactfully holding back to allow mother and son their private moment. "What's all this about Bridget leaving? Surely not!" There was a rare tone in her voice: command.

Markie was still wearing Bridget's rose-colored cardigan, which reached the bottom of his shorts. Caroline looked down at him and laughed. Hand on his head, caressing it, she said, "People who listen by accident, Markie, should sometimes stay for the whole conversation and not just part of it. We went on to way, way ahead when you'd be off to school. Nothing's going to change right now, nothing."

Nothing but everything, Markie thought, still rigid. As soon as that man comes back to the house again. He looked up the stairs at Bridget. It was what she said that would count.

Huff, demeaning ugly word. Don't show one, have one. "We're all civilized people, we'll discuss the matter calmly. Right now I must change my shoes. Perhaps Rose will get Markie a cup of hot cocoa." She turned and went on up the stairs.

"Is this your Ian's work?" Anne asked Caroline.

"Yes, yes," Markie said, "she didn't want to but he—"

"Quiet, Markie. Where is Ian? He went to get you."

"Daddy wouldn't let him. And then Bridget came for me with a taxi."

Caroline didn't like the look on Anne's face, the narrowing of her eyes, the flare of her small fine nostrils.

Possessively, she removed the capacious sweater from her son and hung it on the newel post. "Come along, Markie, we'll see to your cocoa. I'll make it myself for a welcome-home party."

"It makes me suspect her loyalties may lie with Kells." In spite of his mixing up sequences, Markie had displayed what sounded in the taxi like total recall. Quoting a little later, as if he didn't understand it but here it was, as spoken, ". . . he's male, she's female. There may be tale-bearing . . . when she goes off to him in New York . . ."

Bridget sat by the window trying to get her world back to rights. If Ian and Caroline saw her, in a light that scalded, as clinging to her job, a hopeful wench waiting to get her hands on Kells, it would be next to impossible anyway, no matter how much smoothing over was done.

She felt chilled and shaken. Which was to come first, her own basic pride or the child's welfare? "My idea . . . a competent woman . . ." There were plenty of competent women about. Just pass along to Mrs. Blank that peaches made him violently ill, and that when he most mourned and missed his father, right after having to leave him to go to his mother, modeling clay helped tremendously. He was very good, already very talented, with his hands, this of course from his father. He's quite a good little boy, Mrs. Blank. *He's a sweet child and I love him dearly, Mrs. Blank.*

"Tale-bearing. . . ." Markie's eerily accurate reporting gave her a twisted dark vision of herself. She, coming in from some place labeled Backstairs, nervously wiping imaginary red hands on an unseen apron. "Kells—*Mister* Kells—wait till I tell you what he said to her after she came home from that weekend in Paris."

Affronted was another unpleasant, lowering word. She went to the mirror over the dresser to see if this word could be applied to her, saw the clouded troubled face, and gave her hair a good punishing five minutes with the brush.

David McEvoy was a nice man. If she put her foot down about supervising his socks without a license, he would sigh and marry her.

Or . . . She felt a sudden immense longing for Ireland, the benediction rain, the swans on the little lake in Stephen's Green, the flavor of hot buttered potato cake, the voices making conversational music in the air. It would be lovely, to go home. For a while.

Run away home. Run away from Markie. *To hell with you, Markie my boy. Sink or swim, it's all the same to me.*

But this wasn't her voice speaking. This was someone else, a stranger, an affronted skivvy.

The knock on her bedroom door was a welcome interruption. Anne came in, thrusting an embarrassed hand through her cockatoo crest. "I don't know what this is, Bridget," she said, "but if you'll look the other way and stay on for a time I'll give you a bonus of five hundred pounds for each six months."

"Thank you. But it wouldn't be for money, my staying, and I'm afraid it's not my decision. Or yours."

"That man. I don't know . . ." And then to Bridget's amusement—(not before the staff)—she checked herself. "Of course, I'm not marrying him and neither are you." Turning, she added, "The money's there even though you don't, bless you, want it."

"Oh, how nice," Caroline said when Mrs. Orme appeared with the florist's box which had just been delivered at the kitchen entrance.

"They're for Bridget. And where might she be?"

"I'll take them up to her," Markie said. "She must have changed her shoes by this time."

"Probably sulking. All right, little delivery boy."

His heart was considerably lighter. Making the cocoa, she had under single-minded attack from him promised, *promised* that Bridget would remain for a while. "A while" was all he needed for his own purposes; he could stretch it comfortably into forever.

He found her looking through the portfolio of her drawings and watercolors, which he thought more beautiful and worthy than anything he had ever seen in a museum. Because she had done them all by herself.

Wanting her happy, wanting to feel the accustomed easy warmth that wasn't now surrounding her, he said, "Someone sent you flowers. May I stay and watch you open them, may I?"

Her reaction interested him. Pleasure at the dewy white small roses and greenish-white buds in their nest of silky mauve paper, and then reading the note which she took out of a little white envelope— A curious thing, he couldn't remember having seen it before, a pink color flooding her face and throat, sudden, startling.

"Are they from David?" He knew and liked David. The three of them had once had a picnic lunch at Holland Park, and David had imitated the peacock's cry so successfully that it came over to within a foot of him, head to one side like a puzzled dog's.

Bridget, who was normally truth itself and who had instilled a great deal of this quality in her charge, looked him in the eye and said, "Yes."

Key word being indispensable, she mused to herself. But she put the note in its envelope into the drawer that held her scarfs and gloves.

"How do you see it?" Maisie asked, lifting the lid of her sandwich and giving the smoked salmon slices a liberal squeeze of lemon. She had just rather doubtfully made her statement about people keeping their lives in compartments. "He tells no one so it won't leak back to patron Jessica until the deed is done, marriage vows taken?"

That was what had first occurred to Kells. You could live two lives, or three, or four, in a city of twelve million people. You could be Jessica's Ian here and Caroline's Ian there.

"I don't know either of them so it's just a blind guess," he said. "I don't like Queen very much, do you?" Maybe someday he would be a casual sort of uncle to Markie, Peter Queen.

"I like him in a way, but that's because rogues appeal to one streak of me," Maisie said. "Speaking of roguery, you can drop me and my drawing at Pruitt and Cream on the way back to Gerald and Kells Incorporated."

Inspector Rupert Bain of the London Metropolitan Police entered the reception room of Pruitt and Cream thirty seconds before Maisie did.

He went to the desk, introduced himself to Dorothy Williams, showed his credentials and said, "I'd like to see one of the principals."

"*Police*," said Dorothy in a high disbelieving voice as the door opened to admit Maisie. "But I don't . . . Are you interested in renting, or selling? Or buying?"

"No, just looking for a little information." Pruitt and Cream was a weary halfway down a list of hundreds of places and people to cross-check.

Maisie sat down in the chair near the door, and opened a magazine as if she weren't at all interested or even aware of the fact that Scotland Yard was about seven feet away from her.

"Mrs. Cleat is out showing a property, and Mr. Milford won't be in until later," Dorothy said. "Perhaps I could help you?"

"Thank you, I don't think so."

"Well then, Mr. Teller—he's due back from lunch any minute now. He is our junior member."

"I'll wait." Bain sat down in the other chair and because Maisie smiled at him smiled back at her before picking up a copy of the *Spectator*.

She went to the desk with her envelope. "This is for Mrs. Cleat, a drawing she wants." She had wondered about pursuing the matter, now that she had laid eyes on Ian Milford; that had been what her first visit here was all about. But she was driven by a great curiosity, no longer just on Kells' behalf. Who would dream a respectable house agent's office could be such a hotbed? A strong whiff of boiling hatred, and of interesting adultery, in the morning. And police in the afternoon.

As she went out the door, Anthony Teller came in. He was a short, compact, wirily built young man, olive brown as if just back from some sunny palm-treed place. Both his hair and eyes were dark and shining. Dorothy got out the visitor's name and rank as he was rising from his chair. It sounded like an apology from her.

"Come along, Inspector Bain." He looked cheerful but puzzled. In his office, Bain took a comfortable chair to one side of the desk; Pruitt and Cream evidently did not believe in the face-to-face desk encounter which seemed to place the person in the other chair at an automatic disadvantage.

"First of all, who owns this firm?" Bain knew perfectly well who owned it, he had looked up his facts, but he wanted to see if he would meet evasiveness.

"Lord Montroy. It's been a Montroy property for, oh, eighty years, along with dozens of other rather larger interests."

If the Montroys could be considered to be thieves, it was on a far vaster scale, and long ago, centuries; he doubted that they had anything to do with the matter in hand. Lady Jessica though; a dangerous woman in other ways; he knew of her and didn't particularly like what he knew.

Bain got down to business. In early February, there had been a robbery at Kennet Hall in Cambridgeshire, furniture and objects of art valued by the owners at several hundred thousand pounds taken. In June, at Mendy Castle near Dundee, Scotland, the famous Bed of Mendy had been stolen, along with a Jacobean secretary and a rare globe. In September, there had been a robbery of French and English antiques from Dolby Manor in Dolby, Wilts.

"Do you recognize any of the locations?" he asked Teller. He didn't add that the thin and perhaps misleading connecting link had only emerged by the sheerest accident while investigations were going on at Dolby Manor.

"Mmmm—first of all, may I ask *you* a question? Why us?"

"I'll answer that later if you don't. Locations?"

"I remember Mendy, I believe it was on our books, I can check and see who bought it but I still don't see—"

"Who handled the sale, do you know? Which person here?"

"Ian Milford." Teller smiled faintly. "He gets the plums. I'm in a smaller line of goods. Would you be interested, Inspector, in a nice ten-unit apartment dwelling in St. John's Wood? A fine piece of investment property."

He was obviously still puzzled, but unworried and in an amiable mood, which was fine for him but not promising for Bain.

"All three of the properties where the robberies took place were listed with you and no other firm, Mr. Teller."

Eyebrows raised, "And if they were? Are you suggesting that P and C backs up trucks in the dark of night and makes off with the contents of our clients' houses?" He laughed. "But what a good idea now that I come to think of it."

Then he put on a serious face. "Sorry to be frivolous. From where I sit, I would say coincidence. It's a very gilt-edged list, ours, and a very large one always. A sort of Who's Who or Where's Where of stately homes."

Bain, coming here, had thought the same thing and still did, but a good part of his work consisted of turning over the highly unlikely and looking at the underside of it.

This young man appeared to him open and clean-handed, however. He stood up. "I would like a copy of your current list, if you will. And you might give me Milford's home address if he's away from the office a great deal."

"Chelsea Cloisters, that whopper hotel-apartment place on Sloane Avenue. And here," pulling out a desk drawer, "is your list. Good luck, Inspector. Next thing, they'll be making off with the orb and scepter."

NINE

Bridget at Emlyn Court seemed for the time being as inaccessible as Rapunzel in her tower.

He could hardly go striding into the house, waving his arms and commanding all and sundry to do his bidding. And he couldn't start another Markie thunderstorm there. The house was, right now, out of bounds.

It had been a mistake, of course, to tell Caroline he'd have her head if she dispensed with Bridget. Some fences must be mended, and as soon as possible. To be denied access to, contact with, what had brought him here wouldn't do at all.

Invited on his return to the agency to sit in on a three-o'clock meeting during which strategy for Streatham's new Speedfoam Rug Magic would be discussed, he said mendaciously that he'd like to, as soon as he made a telephone call.

Don't overdo it. Caroline knew him too well. "I have an invitation for you. I would have produced it earlier but the morning sort of blew apart, didn't it?"

Would she and Ian dine with him tonight at the Connaught, or any other place that took her fancy? It would be nice to meet Ian in a leisurely way and on a non-emergency basis, he added.

That would be fun, that would be lovely, Caroline told him. Yes, the Connaught, perhaps the grill? Switching subjects, she explained almost defensively that Markie had admitted dismissing his tutor, which was how he had been able to make his dash. "We'll discuss the Bridget thing tonight but right now the status quo looks like the best idea."

She was almost sure Ian was free. She'd call him back before five if he wasn't. "We'll meet you there, when? All right, seven."

If, Kells thought, following the flight of Maisie's fancy, he is not obligated this evening to Lady Jessica Montroy.

After the Speedfoam meeting in his office, Axel said to Ben Voight, "One always has a well-founded belief that one is boring Gerald into the next world with these research findings. You know how he gets up and prowls. Odd thing, the brother seemed completely absorbed, attended to every word."

He was not, Kells reminded himself in the seat he had taken on the broad cushioned windowsill, in the morals business.

However, a new marriage could blow apart with a resounding crash if another, entrenched woman emerged from her shadows. Caroline was possessive in the extreme. But then most people in love were.

"We need not bother our heads with the eight-point-two per cent of our sample who said Speedfoam was no better than plain water for getting out stains," said Lisa Schmidt of Research. She had the required Austrian accent and heavy glasses and disorderly hair which projected the near-psychiatric image cultivated by the well-paid in her field. Good, she thought, that nice Kells Cavanaugh had a piece of paper in his hand, probably for jotting down notes; unlike Gerald, who at this point in the meeting would be lighting one cigarette from another.

Maisie, passing him in the hall on his way to the meeting, had put the little folded piece of paper in his pocket.

"There was a policeman at P and C when I dropped in there," she had written. "Plainclothes—and not bad ones either. As they say on memos around here, F.Y.I."

The handwriting in purple ink was jaunty. Maisie was enjoying herself if no one else was. Police. A traffic violation? No, not plainclothes. Kells found himself deliberately un-

derplaying it. Enough was enough: a titled employer-mistress
—maybe.

They must have many an untenanted house on their list
and as in all great cities vandalism, break-ins were too common to make any sort of news unless whole blocks were plun-
dered, fired and destroyed. A broken window, a smashed door
lock in some house on some expensive street or square.

He crumpled the note but kept it anyway. To go back to
the other matter—quarreling, violence erupting around Markie.
Unless, and of course it was the prudent and obvious thing to
do, Milford would now leave his financially unnecessary job
with Pruitt and Cream. He wouldn't be needing a job of any
kind anymore.

The rain had turned heavy and cold; it was nice to get in
out of it. Besides, the firm not running to secretaries, Dorothy
kept a daily diary of the staff's entrances and exits, times and
places, in order that they might be reached if important calls
came in for them. It wasn't a bad thing to appear in a bustle
in Dorothy's book. Ian had no idea if they were saved or
thrown away or even looked at after the day and date when
in use.

"Hello, Mr. Milford," Dorothy said. "Let's see, four-ten."

Tony Teller, halfway into his raincoat, appeared at the corridor entrance. "Garner house, Hampstead Heath, the number's on my desk, Dorothy." And to Ian, "Can't stop now, but
the police have been here—singular, that is, an inspector—"
and with his three-cornered grin, "wanting to know if you
stole the Bed of Mendy. Must run. They'll be getting in touch
with you later, they say." The front door closed behind him.

Before Dorothy's gaze, as always eager and admiring, Ian
contained his face and allowed himself to show no interest
whatever in Teller's flippant declaration. He went into his
office, took off his wet coat and sat down at his desk. Three
messages, but make his own call first.

At Queen's Taste, Hans Baum answered the telephone. He
expected Peter no later than fiveish, he said.

Ian made short work of his three business calls and reached for his coat. No point in sitting here. "They'll be getting in touch with you later, they say." Five, ten, fifteen minutes from right now? Before he'd had a chance to talk to Peter? Before he could even find out if they'd been to Peter, first?

He was crossing the reception room—"I'm off and away for the day, Dorothy"—when a light flashed on her desk indicator. "Call for you, Mr. Milford, will you take it in your office?"

In his haste, he left his office door a little open on his return. Mrs. Cleat, having just come in out of the rain herself, was making her dripping way along the corridor; she had given her ankle a bit of a twist getting off the bus from Pimlico.

"Hello, Caro darling, I'm in an almighty-to-Christ hurry, what—?" Short listening silence. His ear, and Mrs. Cleat's.

Hatred, like love, has a special way of understanding nuances, its antennae most exquisitely tuned and ready. Not a social voice, his, now, although he was in a hurry. A personal voice. "Well yes, I'd like that. I suppose. Seven, did you say? I'll be round to you before then and we'll have some time for ourselves first. By the way, your gloves are still in my pocket, all ten delightful fingers of them."

Mrs. Cleat slipped into the nearest empty office, Tony Teller's, and waited quietly. Caro. Darling. *Who, where?* Ankle or not, there was only one way to find out.

Taxi-waiting under the circumstances, rain, offices emptying, streets filling, slowed baying traffic, was not to be borne. Ian walked to Hyde Park Corner and went by the Underground to Earl's Court. Emerging, he turned left on Earl's Court Road, crossed the Cromwell Road, and continued north toward Kensington High Street.

He found himself grateful for the anonymity, the slight tattiness of the neighborhood. Sidewalks not so crowded, wet mournfully dripping trees, alternating bright streetlit glare and rainswept darkness.

To reach Queen's Taste, you turned into a shabby narrow high-walled brick walkway, the sign "Rooks Mews" half concealed by the growth of the wall ivy. The walkway led to a cobble-stoned yard. On the left was a small low house, pale blue when there was enough light to see the color, balconied, half buried in ivy and further shielded and shrouded in the waving branches of weeping willows.

Fronting squarely across the center of the yard was a long, low, meandering building with erratic wings and extensions rambling backward. There was a wide cobbled drive on its left side, and a loading platform. Access to the driveway was from Lever's Lane, which ran behind the rear of the warehouse. Daylight would show the mildly down-at-heels condition of the premises, the long dying grass against the walls, the dusty wired glass of the windows, the stands of dock and nettles, the stains of oil on the stones. But the small shop across the front of the building was spruce enough. Shining many-paned bow windows, a pale blue door, a sign swinging in the wind, nicely lettered, black on white: "Queen's Taste, Export-Import, Wholesale & Retail."

The combination showroom-shop was still lighted. All else was in darkness. Ian went in to the clang of a bell hanging on the doorknob. Shelved merchandise winked and glowed and stared at him. China and glass, straw and wicker and pottery, plastic and earthenware, wool and silk and synthetics, macramé; from Hong Kong, Manila, Mexico, India, Yugoslavia, Italy, Portugal, Taiwan, Japan, the People's Republic of China.

A door at the back of the shop opened at the sound of the bell and Hans Baum appeared. He was in his forties, short and ramrod-straight, bald, with large soft blue eyes in a face as rigidly boned as his body. He had been with Peter since Salisbury. Part high-class servant, part professional assistant, and part—Ian thought but wasn't sure and wasn't interested —occasional lover. In any case he had shown over the years an inflexible loyalty to Peter Queen.

("Is Hans all right?" Ian had asked long ago. "As right as the flag, home, and mother," Peter said. "And throw in Gibraltar while you're at it.")

"Evening, Hans, Peter around yet?"

"He may have come in and gone right to the house. You know how he is." The fact that the house was dark didn't necessarily mean Peter wasn't there. He liked when the mood took him to sit for hours on end, without lights, listening to his favorite symphonies on an elaborate stereo system.

But Ian, passing the house, had heard no leak of music. Go and check, anyway. Before he left the shop, innate caution asserted itself. "Give me a dozen of this Waterford liqueur." He paid for them and pocketed the receipt while Hans carefully wrapped each little glass.

What took you to Queen's Taste, Mr. Milford? I wanted to pick up a little gift for my aunt-in-law-to-be, Miss Anne Eldredge.

Carrying the box, he crossed the yard to Peter's doorstep. Double knock, pause, then single, pause, then double again. After a wait of perhaps a minute, the door opened inward. From a little distance away, Peter's voice said, "Come in."

Something about the sound of the voice made him hesitate. But only for the drawing of a breath. He walked boldly in, remembering not to bump into the big desk on his close right. He sensed but couldn't see motion, and then with a low-flying shoulder and arm striking his knees went crashing to the floor, Peter half on top of him, wiry powerful body, smothering reek of brandy.

"For Christ's *sake!*" Ian was the stronger of the two, and sober. He shoved Peter aside and got up and turned on the green-shaded student's lamp on the desk. Peter lay propped on his elbow, blinking, and then slowly rose and stuffed his shirt back into his trousers.

"Sorry. I've been brooding, I suppose. You've hurt my feelings, did you know that?" He opened a desk drawer and took out a Smith & Wesson .38. Nothing new about the gun; he'd had this one since a smash-and-grab at the warehouse a year ago.

He stood looking at it and said, "Tell me all about Caroline. And do get it straight. I can check all the details with Kells Cavanaugh, I *think* that was his name."

"Put that thing down. In the condition you're in you might shoot off a toe. Yours wouldn't matter but mine would." Under the surface calm he felt himself pinned, with no verbal escape route. Try, anyway.

"You know her name, so that's covered. She wanted to keep things secret until we married. Family complications."

"Disinheritance hovering? Nameless adventurer from Rhodesia after someone's darling daughter? Money, then— Tell me all."

Thank you, Peter.

"Something like that."

"English, American? Blond, dark? Divorced, I'm told. Children? Where does she live?"

"I don't see what any of that's got to do with you."

"Don't you?" A wave of the gun. "I don't see secrets between friends as Siamese-close as we are. It makes me nervous. I've had none from you and up till now you've had—that I know of—none from me."

Stay calm. It was all right, almost, except for the great black cloud sending out forked lightning. If Peter went maliciously to Jessica . . .

"American. One child, a boy, six. She lives in Mayfair when she's not in New York." She wasn't listed in the directory. Peter would have no way of finding her. If he had any reason for doing so.

"Good show. Instant family, moneyed." Peter laughed a little. "As I said, close friends should be open with one another. It pays. Anyone else but me might think of this as another hold over you. Or two, throwing in the blushing bride herself. But thanks for baring your breast. Finally." He put the gun back in the drawer.

Ian's gaze, allowing itself the first removal from the gun, the hand holding it, found his own face in the mirror over the desk. Blood trickling from his cheekbone, where he'd been slammed against a chair leg. Purple bruise no doubt to follow.

Time for a shift in the balance of power. Peter's dramatics had made him forget briefly his errand here.

"I came by to tell you that a police inspector apparently paid a visit to P and C this afternoon. I was out. He talked to our junior partner."

"What did he talk to him about?" Peter's eyes looked sharply focused, and sobered.

"He didn't report the whole conversation to me, he was on his way out. He did mention the Bed of Mendy."

"Are you sure this isn't out of the whole cloth? Sweet revenge for being floored just now? Knuckles rapped. Mind your manners, Peter, or you're in the soup for good. But no, on second thought it's a two-way street you and I are on. Soup pot for two is perhaps what I mean."

"I'll go wash my face while you think it over. And pour me a drink, will you."

When he came back from the bathroom he found Peter quieted, pouring brandy into two glasses. "Thanks for coming by. Probably the beginning and end of it in any case. A routine check at P and C and every other house agent in the city —or the country. Not necessarily for a culprit, but for any possibly helpful guesses, or information that might lead to et cetera et cetera."

"Glad to see you've cooled down," Ian said. "But don't be too stride-taking about it. You might need your adrenaline."

Peter shrugged. "As I see it, no problem. *If* there is one, real, they'll be checking every antiques dealer in London and the Continent, and the States. And if they can find the money and the men, the Middle East and Russia. To say nothing of South America."

He lifted his glass. "Sorry, you had me worried, back there a bit, and I let go with a crash. Here's," after a sip of brandy, "to the man in the clear. Can I give you dinner? Cold stuffed game hens in the fridge, Hans did them."

"No, I'm due to look at a—" Ian emptied half his glass and dropped into the language of house agents' ads—"dignified town residence, two recep, circ stairway, wine c, four wood-b fireplaces, four bed, three b, walled g. Cheyne Walk."

"You should be able to afford a place like that any day now. Will I be invited there?"

"What a silly question." Ian smiled and finished his brandy.

On his way out of Rooks Mews, he thought it was probably time to finish all this.

The "If you don't, I won't" and "If you will, I will" had worked well enough but he couldn't see it as a forever partnership.

Especially now, especially with Caroline to be folded into his life. (Where and how in Christ had Peter run across Kells Cavanaugh? Or should the names be reversed, in that question? Must track that down.)

And Peter's games-playing, his treacherous streak, might accentuate with time, as many almost buried characteristics have a way of doing.

I have two more holds over you now, he had pointed out, laughing.

No, it wouldn't work at all, when the perilous equality of the two of them was altered.

Across the road and down a little from the entrance to Rooks Mews was a coffee shop, not yet crowded. They did serve tea on request, to Mrs. Cleat's tired relief. Her ankle throbbed. It hadn't been easy even without that disadvantage to keep up with Ian, the wet sidewalks, umbrellas to dodge with her own, the steeply pitched escalator in the Hyde Park Corner Underground station, which made her feel a little dizzy.

If by any chance he happened to spot her at the far end of the car, she would explain then or later that she was on her way to Richmond. Richmond was the final destination of the train they both switched to at the South Kensington Station.

It was easier on dark rainy Earl's Court Road, although his pace was still fast. She kept well back and there is nothing like a black umbrella held forward against the wind for obscuring a head and face.

Was it this mews where he was going to join his darling? Seven, he had said. It was only five-twenty now. But they were to have some time by themselves first, before something else. Or was this a stop, an errand, on the way to her?

From her little table by the window, she had an unobstructed view of the mews entrance. But what if there was an exit at the back? What if, after hours and hours of waiting on her part, he didn't appear at all?

Oh well, she had Rooks Mews. It wouldn't be the first time that she had knocked on the door of a strange house and said, entering and offering her card, "What a charming house. I'm told it's for sale. Is that correct? Oh, sorry, my mistake."

After three cups of tea, she saw Ian come out carrying a square white box. She had already paid her check, just in case, and was standing near the glass-paned door by the cashier's desk in the attitude of an impatient woman, glancing often at her watch, waiting to be picked up here by prearrangement.

He walked down to the Cromwell Road, she half a block behind him. The British Airways Terminal was a short distance east on the Cromwell Road, and empty taxis were heading hopefully for it as well as passenger-bearing ones. Ian got his immediately and Mrs. Cleat hers four seconds later. It sounded odd, like something from an old film, but she said it anyway: "Please follow that cab just ahead, but do stay behind it."

The driver turned to look at her when both cabs stopped for a red light. Private detective, maybe? He wouldn't like to have her on *his* trail if she was.

When the first taxi turned into Emlyn Court from Sloane

Avenue, he said, "Cul-de-sac, no way through. What now? Your party is—yes, he wants that house at the end."

Mrs. Cleat paid hastily and got out at the corner. She hobbled halfway up the court on the narrow sidewalk. She was in time, with her keen and hungry sight, to see the wide front door of the white Palladian house open. Light, warmth, color, comfort in the cold wet night. Just the merest glimpse of the young woman before Ian, his back to her view, his trench coat swinging wide, bent to kiss the woman as with one hand he closed the door behind him.

House number, 24. In her elation, Mrs. Cleat decided to press her luck. She went into a small tobacconist's shop two doors up from the corner and registered distressed confusion to the girl behind the counter.

"Oh dear, I think I'm lost. I thought my new friend Mrs. Benson lived in the big house at the end of the court but—"

"Oh, no, that's Miss Eldredge's," the girl said. "She's lived here twenty years or more."

Mrs. Cleat ventured on. "But I thought I saw a *young* woman going in, and Mrs. Benson has a niece, you're sure . . . ?"

"That would be Miss Eldredge's niece," the girl said patiently. "American. Staying there with her little boy. No, really, you have the wrong house and I don't know of any Benson in the Court unless they're new."

"Thank you so much." Mrs. Cleat bought a box of thin chocolate-covered peppermint creams. "I must just go to the telephone box and look her up in the directory again. You have been most helpful."

TEN

"Ian, your poor *cheek.*" A tender forefinger touching his skin an inch away from the small plastic strip bandage, dull livid color beginning to show around it.

As they went into the drawing room, left empty for them, he explained the cheek. "Mugged, of all things, in the Underground. A crowd, someone tripped me up—why do people say trip *up* when it's *down* you go?—and on my descent to the platform I struck my face against a peanut-vending machine. A dashing performance in every way. The other of the pair helped me up and while doing so helped himself to my billfold."

"Of course you went to the police?"

"Might as well report a bee sting in St. James Park." He laughed lightly. "Naturally I did, they were very nice, warned me never to flaunt my money in public, which I never do. And if it's turned in at the station they'll mail it to me. Anyway, I won't need it tonight, with your former husband picking up the tab. Let's both order caviar to start, shall we?"

The Connaught Hotel, on Carlos Place, was only a short distance away from the office; no point in going all the way back to his own hotel to change.

The big, busy office thrumming by day was quiet now, Friday-night quiet, emptied early and decisively for the weekend. Just one remote typewriter, the long silences between the hesitant clackings giving the effect of yawns; and from far down the hall, the sound of a sheet of paper being torn from a large pad. Ben Voight, probably, evicted from his Head Art Director's office, hard at work on roughs for introductory newspaper ads on Speedfoam. Axel, at the end of the afternoon meeting, had said in menacing shorthand, "By Monday morning, Ben?" "Yes, of course, what on earth else would *I* have to amuse myself with on Saturday and Sunday?"

Kells had thought about giving him back his office and then decided against it. In the world as it was now, you got nowhere, in fact went backward, by being accommodating, tossing away your status, such as it was. Don't mind me, I'm just Kells.

He had, however, offered to help on Rug Magic. "Between the two of us we ought to make a pile high enough to let you off the hook on Sunday."

He worked at his own extraordinary natural speed at the drawing board. As a beginner, fresh out of art school, he had had to be removed from a bull pen of four young art directors because his pace so unnerved the others, and given a cubbyhole to himself. It was not a matter of quantity over quality. He was one of the half-dozen best-known men in his field in New York, for the style, strength and originality of his talent.

"Oh my, oh bless me," Maisie said, looking over his shoulder at six o'clock. She bent and kissed the back of his neck, a warm blossomy touch against the skin. "Why didn't you tell me how marvelous you are? Will you do me some Go Soap things when you have ten minutes or so?"

He was sorely tempted to get up and kiss her back and start something after the long loneliness; a self-imposed loneliness that he didn't entirely understand. But he smiled instead and said yes he would and where was she off to?

"As you haven't bespoken me, I'm going to spend the evening with a bunch of tearaways. What did you think of my policeman?"

"I thank you for him, but he was probably collecting for the British equivalent of the Police Benevolent Association."

"You're being two-headed, aren't you? One head doesn't

want there to be anything sinister, not to say dangerous or even criminal, about your child's new papa."

Shrewd Maisie. "Out of the mouths of babes," he said agreeingly.

"I'm, what? only ten or so years younger than you are." She managed to look both worldly and indignant. "Will you take me out somewhere, sometime tomorrow, and buy me a balloon?"

"I'll try, I'll call you in any case." His new, devoted and highly efficient right-hand man. Perhaps he could get over this odd holding back of himself by tomorrow.

Even in a hotel where famous faces, international faces, and the occasional royal countenance were not uncommon, Caroline and Ian made a silent wave when they walked down the steps from the lobby into the Connaught Grill.

Caroline was wandlike, obviously herself but still a part of the man, in thin violet silk which seemed blown against her body by an invisible breeze, no jewelry except a flicker of diamond tassels hanging from her earlobes. Ian, tall, his carriage commanding and self-assured, his coloring as of a man seen in a cold moonlit landscape. The small and now unbandaged red mark and bruise on his cheekbone somehow gave the startling underlining effect of a beauty spot.

Kells got up from the round corner table he had reserved. All very festive, a low crystal bowl of roses on the glistening white cloth, a little wrapped box at Caroline's place. A present bought on the way back from the pub, to be offered as having been in his pocket and forgotten, brought over from New York.

Without intending propitiation, or bowing or bending, he wanted a relationship with the two, for the time being, that the Entwhistles of the world would no doubt call viable. He had to have access to Markie, and Bridget; to Caroline and, if wanted, to Ian. Opposing armed camps, his one- (or two-) man operation wouldn't suit his purpose at all.

Caroline at first seemed to go along with the idea of

civilized sociability. Yes, martinis, lovely. What was this mysterious little box? Oh Kells, how sweet. The bracelet was neither expensive nor inexpensive, a thin hoop of gold, gadroon-edged. Caroline collected bracelets.

When the drinks came, Kells lifted his and said, "Obvious, but—to both of you. To your happiness."

Caroline sipped and leaned across the table and touched Kells' hand. "First and foremost, to clear the air and let us party at peace, I talked to Bridget and got this silly misunderstanding all straightened out. Naturally Markie won't need her when he goes to school but that's not for at least a year."

"Good." He still had to talk to Bridget. He had promised her with his roses that he would. But, in the meantime, continue the easy and almost comfortable talk. Kells saw that when Ian was pleasant he could be very pleasant indeed. An amusing story or two about houses and clients, short and pointed; they laughed and were merry.

Picking up his second drink, Kells wondered fleetingly what would happen if he declaimed: "To absent friends. Jessica Montroy for one." Probably nothing; Ian did not at the moment look vulnerable.

And in fact sounded casual when he asked, "I gather you bumped into an acquaintance of mine, Peter Queen, where?"

"A pub, the Swallow. The girl I was with knew him." His tone was equally casual. Don't give him what would amount to a kick under the table: funny thing, he had no idea you were going to be married. Poor public relations right now.

Caroline shot Ian a wicked intimate glance as they looked at menus. "No, darling. The saumon fumé, we both love it." One drink was her usual preference. Kells saw that the extra measure was getting to her. Or perhaps not solely the gin and vermouth, but the surrounding eyes on them, she all violet and ivory, gently glowing from within; and two, yes, all right, attractive men all to herself. And then, the delicious enjoyment of showing one man to the other. You see, I'm wanted, loved, and isn't he fabulous?

How, she wanted to know, was Gerald and his family? And

was it some dreadful emergency that had brought Kells to London? "Or just in an Olympian way looking at a campaign for something or other and saying, yes, that's fine, or, no, do it over. What fun it must be to rule roosts."

She captured capers on her fork. "No, it couldn't be an emergency, I still remember you coming in after midnight, all bloodshot, and working through weekends . . . while here you are dining out at dinnertime, visiting the zoo, sitting in Anne's garden drinking sherry."

Her blue dreamer's eyes, lashes half dropped and glistening, met his, and he could suddenly feel her long cool delicate tendrils quietly prying, searching for his nerve ends.

She turned to Ian, mouth curved in laughter. "One is almost tempted to think Kells has come to vet you. Take your measure as husband and father. After all, he just got my letter a week before pressing business summoned him over the Atlantic. If we weren't being so . . . observed, I'd say stand up, Ian dear, and turn around very slowly, and let him see you from all angles. Let him decide if you'll do."

Ian looked, not at her, but across the table at his host, his eyes wholly concentrated, something momentarily odd about the pupils. Kells had no idea how many years it had been since he had blushed, but he felt the blaze under his skin, like a fever attacking without warning.

There was not much he could do about it. They were all aware, and he knew it, that Caroline had tossed the truth on the table. Carelessly, maliciously. And accurately.

Swim with the current, then. "I won't bore you with my labors on Streatham's Speedfoam Rug Magic. But it would be a bit strange if I weren't interested, wouldn't it?"

Ian put a thoughtful finger to his bruised cheek. Dinner now arrived with grace and ceremony. Entrecôte for him and for Caroline; the usual business of lovers wanting to eat the same things. Grilled Dover sole for Kells. Salad of endive, a renewal of pale sweet butter curls in crushed ice. The wine waiter at Kells' elbow, wine settled on, poured.

Ian cut himself a slice of entrecôte and verbally backtracked. "Kells' approval is academic. But as we'll be sharing a son, it's nice to be able to coexist."

Cool and quick-witted of him: straight for the jugular.

Eating his salad, Kells tried to picture Ian as bought and paid for. "Almost like a kept man, except in a respectable office, instead of lying around a boudoir eating chocolates." It wasn't easy. It seemed, here and now, a scheme of Maisie's to comfort, to intrigue. What fun, let's look into this villain.

Before coffee, he excused himself. It was only away from the table that he allowed himself to hear the words again, itching, scalding.

"Sharing a son."

The presumption of it, the impossible gall. The flat reality of it. Literal, in terms of daily living.

He went to the telephone in the lobby and called Anne's house. Rose answered. "Bridget went out to get— No, here she is now."

At the sound of her voice, he felt a sweet gush of relief or happiness under his ribs, enough to take his breath away.

Why?

Oh yes—because it was all right, now, Bridget not saying to hell with it, with all of you, and leaving—

Leaving Markie, who for a while would need her so badly.

"As it was something I was not officially supposed to hear, I could hardly act officially on it," Bridget said. "Caroline bent over backward, said she'd sign a year's contract if I wanted it, which I don't because—" a last faint flare of defiance, or pain —"that would bind me, too."

She went looking for Markie; it was getting time for his bath and bed. He knew about the dinner. Caroline, thinking to institute a firm family warmth and confidence, no barriers, no secrets, had said, "We're meeting Daddy for dinner, Ian and I, doesn't that sound like fun? Give me a kiss on the palm and I'll pat his cheek with it."

Markie had been very quiet over his dinner. Obscurely trying to comfort him, Bridget, sharing the vegetable soup and hot biscuits, said, "You know, you're very like your father. More so every day."

"Am I? I wouldn't leave *him* alone. If he needed me." He put down his spoon. "I'm almost to the bottom of the bowl, Bridget, is that all right?"

Now, searching, she found him hidden but not in a hiding place, concealed by the curving flange of the great wing chair in the drawing room, slowly turning over the pages of a large book filled with colored illustrations of birds. "There you are."

Light from the fire brightened and dimmed on him. Bridget, looking down with love, found herself seeing secret innocent places in a wood, ferns dewed, clear amber brook water flowing by a bank of white violets. Little hazel-eyed animals making the softest rustle in the underbrush, hurting nothing, threatening nothing, wanting only life.

A renewed wave of gold as a top log took fire shone on Markie's minted freshness. His mouth was as much poetry as flesh, grave and sweet. The eyes lifted to hers were a naked soft gray, darkly rimmed with Kells' startlingly thick lashes.

No, I couldn't have left him, she thought, not on my own decision. Not right now, not when he's driven to take shelter in his own private wood.

She had no idea what the look on her face told, but he smiled at her. And with sudden quite normal indignation said, "It says here people used to eat swans. Did they, Bridget? *Swans?*"

"If they did they've long since learned better," Bridget said.

The three had an almost cordial parting at the foot of the Connaught steps. Caroline, after her brief bitch flight, had dropped back into easy charm over their Camembert and ripe apricots and coffee.

"Lovely party," she said over the doorman's cab whistle. She moved close to Ian under his umbrella. "I suppose you, poor thing, will be working tomorrow?"

"For a couple of hours, but I'd like some time with Markie."

To have to ask for Markie. And politely, and in front of Ian Milford.

"Oh dear," Caroline said. "We're all going down to Sussex for the weekend. Ian's never seen Anne's country establishment and the weather report sounds promising. We won't be leaving until ten or thereabouts but please, Kells, don't ring up. You'd only serve to spoil Markie's weekend and ours at one fell swoop. Don't worry about it, I'll tell him you're completely tied up, hand and foot. Oh—blessings on it, here comes our taxi."

ELEVEN

"Take it from me," Lucy Bain said to her husband, "the Bed of Mendy is probably right now in Iran or Iraq or one of those oily places. Six or seven women reclining on it in saris—no, that's India—or whatever they wear or don't wear, waiting for their one-and-only lord and master."

She gave him, amiably, half of her butter-dripping second crumpet and refilled his teacup. "If you track it down, the bed, say you'll shut up if he'll give you a year's worth of heating oil."

Milford hadn't been available last night. Out, unless he wasn't answering the telephone at Chelsea Cloisters, and that seemed unlikely in his line of business.

"I don't see why you can't have your Saturday off. After all, this has been going on since February."

"That's the point. Since February, and I'm ass-on to nowhere."

It was a nice day, mild, with a hint of pale sun coming through cloud. He had himself driven in the police Rover to the gray building rising like a cliff face over Sloane Avenue. As he went up the steps, a man passed him, coming out of one of the two revolving doors flanking the main doors. Tall, striking, someone you'd look at even if you weren't a woman. Country tweeds, heather mix, expensive. Tattersall shirt, dark red wool tie knotted in the plump jut Bain had never been quite able to achieve. Glossy leather duffel bag.

With a flash of precognition, Bain thought, I wonder if that could be—

Not liking any more than a layman to look impulsive,

foolish, he failed to act on instinct. The handsome man, evidently not in need of a cab, turned right and strode briskly down the street.

At the deserted desk, Bain waiting impatiently. Help these days, slack. Finally the door behind the desk opened and a jaunty uniformed black man came out. Mr. Ian Milford's apartment number—yes, sir. Take the elevator at the rear. Bain could have used the house telephone in the lobby but didn't want to herald his arrival.

Getting out on the sixth floor, he was reminded by the length and angling of the corridor of air terminal passage-ways. Huge place, this. Not out-of-sight expensive as far as he remembered; an aunt of Lucy's had lived here a few years back.

Number 677. He was passing 669 when, a good way up the corridor, he saw a woman, head bent, searching her big pouched handbag. She was three-quarters to him and he got a good sharp view. This time he knew for certain, from news-paper and magazine photographs, whom he was looking at.

Tall, with a honed limberness to her in the lean black jersey pullover suit. Black hair, a great deliberately undisciplined rise and sweep of it. She sent at him a blaze of health, of powered fitness and sun-burnished skin, which in this city of pallors and bronchial disorders he found himself resenting. Raking shape to the wide mouth, bold nose for a woman but a well-made one, something imperious about the nostrils.

She found the key she had obviously been looking for and inserted it in the lock. No knock, no ring—but surely she didn't live here, or have quarters here? He moved swiftly. She was going into 677.

"Well, that makes two of us," he said, right behind her. She turned in the open doorway. Beyond her he saw the one-room studio flat, bright colors, reasonably tidy, empty. Unless Mil-ford was in the bathroom.

"Who in hell are you?" asked Lady Jessica Montroy.

No point, this early on, in plastering a "police inquiries" label on the man; or at least in front of this woman. "Bain,

Rupert Bain, thought I'd see if he was free this fine Saturday morning." He knew he didn't particularly look like police: thin, a little stooped, and with a deceptive mild scholarly look.

She went to what must be the bathroom door, knocked lightly, and listened with her head cocked. Bain listened too. No splashing, flushing. Silence.

She gave him a glance of brief fury. "Our bird has flown. Where's his engagement book? Here—" She flipped owningly through it. "Nothing, God damn him. Oh well." She crossed the room and closed the front door behind her.

"Nothing" was well put. A search wasn't indicated, and he hadn't a warrant. Milford might come back at any moment. Bain had noted the side doors of the lobby on his way to the rear, and the back entrance, where private cars could be pulled up.

Comfortable here. Milford must have added some things of his own, some of the furniture looked elegant, expensive, and personal. Not one of the pieces, though—Bain smiled faintly at himself after the careful survey—was on his list of stolen property. A bowl of fresh fruit between tall candles on the round white dining table. Bed left every which way for the maid to make—as he recalled they had maid service here thrown in with the rent. An open book on the long white shelves separating the bed area from the sitting and living space. Nancy Mitford's *The Sun King*. Silk foulard robe thrown over a straight chair. A smell, pleasant, a bit gingery, perhaps cologne splashed on.

Nothing.

The day manageress, an attractive and very busy young woman, showed no surprise when he identified himself. In a place this size, she might well be used to police. Thefts, the building itself was a warren; and when you put in excess of a thousand people under one roof there must occasionally be trouble.

Her answers were crisp and concise. Ian Milford had been a tenant for a little under a year. No, no problems with him, no wild parties, complaints from neighbors along the hall. His rent was £140 a month, not inconsistent, Bain thought, with the probable income of a man in his line. No, he didn't own a car or if he did he didn't garage it here. Single, or at least the apartment was in his name only. "One can't help wondering why," she observed, smiling. "Stunning, absolutely. Of course, he may keep an interchangeable harem up there. One of the things people like about this place is privacy." And, no, she had no evidence one way or another whether he was a heavy spender of money on occasion.

"You mean cases of champagne delivered, rose trees and orchids being carried up in the elevators? Nothing that's caught anyone's eye as far as I know." She had no idea who his friends and associates might be in case Inspector Bain wanted to get in touch with them. "He gives me an impression of being rather a private man."

So far, Bain told himself sourly on leaving, Ian Milford had managed to retain from the police point of view total privacy. Except for the fact that, with his employer Jessica Montroy, he must be on what couldn't be less than intimate terms.

In the hall Anne encountered Markie, coming out of the bathroom. He was dressed for the Bentley journey to Sussex in gray flannel shorts and jacket, white linen shirt, gray knee socks and new shoes. When he saw her, he lifted a shielding forearm over his eyes.

Crying, in there, in the bathroom. Snatched away by high-handed adults from any possible contact with his father for at least two days. "Well, we've been talking about it for weeks," Caroline had said. "Do let's go to the country tomorrow. Ian's dying to see Alton Hall. And it will be fun to take care of my own child without benefit of Bridget."

Blast Caroline. Blast Ian Milford. Too bad her loved sister Cecelia hadn't lived longer; she had died so fresh and young, undeveloped, that Anne had no idea whom and what she would turn into, and couldn't apply any known clues to Cecelia's daughter Caroline. I know her but I don't know her.

How could she possibly want a man like Milford?

She bent to Markie. Try to stop up a wound. Make it any-one's fault but his own mother's. She wanted to say "darling" but didn't know how. Female-to-male softness was beyond her capacity. Daughter of a hated, towering, unkind father, she had been since childhood terrified of men. Except Kells. Kells was dear, even if he was a man.

To Kells' son, she said, "It's all my fault. There are a dozen things that have to be done in my garden or all hell will break loose." (Should one say hell before a six-year-old child?) Awkwardly, she managed to put an arm about the thin slender shoulders under their gray flannel. Goodness, what light bones. Not much of an underpinning for the vul-nerable flesh.

"The pony's all very well, but I do think, yes—let's have a crack at it—you might be ready for a horse. There's a little bay mare, Hester, who needs exercise, riding up and down the lane. You remember, the one that leads up past the willow grove to the windmill. Tell Bridget to pack your riding things."

Markie lifted his face and gave her a tentative, rescued smile.

"You're overdue for a weekend off," Caroline said to Bridget while Markie's small canvas bag was being packed. "We'll take over for you. Have a fling, dear."

Having no particular desire to spend the weekend in the country, Bridget took her offer at face value. It might be some kind of apology, or lagniappe. Or it might be the beginning of a new phase: gradually easing her out, a few days here, a week there, getting Markie used to thriving happily without her.

As any kind of security had vanished, and as it would never again be the same, the job, she was philosophical about Caroline's possible plots and plans. There would be uninter-rupted time to get at her own work. And time for David's socks. Rose and Mrs. Orme had been given the weekend off too. It would be lovely to have the house to herself.

"Don't forget to feed the birds, Bridget," said Anne.

She was just getting out of a leisurely deep late-morning bath when there was a forthright double drop of the knocker on the front door. Swearing to herself, she took a voluminous white toweling robe off the hook and ran in her wet bare feet down the stairs.

It was Kells, standing just outside in the pale sun. It had occurred to him that the Sussex weekend could have been a put-up story to keep him comfortably at arm's length from Markie, and he had decided to take a small detour on his way to Allory Place to work.

A phone call wouldn't do. Caroline might well say, "Oh, you just caught me in time; we're leaving right now."

He looked with some surprise and a certain pleasure at Bridget's face, which was a steamed pink, and the trickle of water down one wrist. "Have you dried yourself or are you still wet all over? I gather you're the only one here?"

"Still wet. They've all gone off. Didn't Caroline even tell you?"

"Yes, but I didn't know how early. Well, then—" No point in coming in, or was there? He should, now that he was here, have a nice talk with Bridget. Find out how Markie was doing with his tutor, and how his general health had been, and so on. Fatherly concerns.

From somewhere upstairs, her room it must be, floated the surpassing loveliness of the "Siegfried Idyll."

"The draft," Bridget suggested gently, pulling her robe tighter around her.

"Oh, sorry, yes." He came in and closed the door firmly behind him. That hastily scrawled note—it for some reason repeated itself in his mind. "Dear darling indispensable Bridget—"

Would she be thinking that he . . . That he what? She alone in the house, damp naked body under the white robe. Wet lock of dark hair falling across her broad forehead. And he had never seen her barefooted before. Slender feet, straight toes. But then, she was slender all over except for the round lift of her breasts. Nothing like the sturdy girl who had come on the bus from Dublin to be interviewed for a job. Strange he hadn't noticed the slow sweeping change, before this. Bridget was just Bridget, indispensable. Leaving out the other adjectives.

"I don't like to interrupt your train of thought," she said, smiling, "but I must get back upstairs."

Dismissing him, softly and civilly. She'd have a life of her own to pick up or continue with, these two days. Was there a man in it? Of course there would be a man in it.

How inconvenient it would be if, Caroline having been controlled, the man swept Bridget away, to have for himself.

Well, right now, split the difference at a nice safe midpoint. He put his hands on her shoulders and kissed her where the lock of hair touched her left eyebrow.

"Good news, good news!" cried the mynah bird, stamping in what appeared to be excitement up and down his perch.

What were his hands doing still resting on her shoulders, the fingers beginning to tighten a little? He dropped them abruptly.

"Well put," he said to the mynah bird. "That you're going to bear with the lot of us for a while longer, I mean, Bridget. Good-bye, I won't keep you."

Going down the court, he wondered at his own haste in leaving. What had happened to his fatherly questions? They had gone, for just that short space, completely out of his head.

Those turning up at the office for weekend work—or to collect a forgotten umbrella, or in one case to manage a convenient illicit lovers' meeting in Axel's office, which had not one but two great sofas in it—either used their own keys if they were executives or rang the bell for Mr. Poll, if they were staff.

Mr. Poll was a retired policeman approaching seventy,

plump and perennially sleepy. He spent his security weekends at Cavanaugh and Cavanaugh mostly in his comfortable
snug in the basement, where he played Patience, read his
newspaper, drank a great deal of beer, and refreshed himself further with occasional naps on his nice big bed.

Kells had not been provided with a key. A short time after
he had rung, a yawning Mr. Poll opened the door to him and
asked, "Name, sir? Your face isn't—?"

"Cavanaugh. Kells."

"Oh, in that case, consider the place yours. But then it is,
isn't it?" Mr. Poll grinned at his little joke. Wishing to show
efficiency and snap, he sketched a half salute and reported,
"Quiet so far. Mr. Voight in, and Mr. Watters."

Saturday and Sunday offices always fascinated Kells. The
feeling of life suspended but hanging buzzing in the air. Per-
sonalities inhabiting offices like lively ghosts, smells of to-
bacco and perfume and the acrid ink of felt-tipped pens. A
red silk scarf trailing rakishly from a doorknob. One mislaid
pigskin glove apparently found by the cleaning crew and
placed on the seat of a typing chair.

Ben Voight, pleasantly ugly, gnarl-faced, with a shock of
graying fair hair, said from the top of the stairs, "Well, I
never. Kind of you, Kells. Come and see where I've got to and
then you can let loose. I like your last-night thing, I think that
might be it."

Kells' last-night thing was a double-page newspaper spread,
the right-hand page occupied top to bottom with the powerful and elegant lettering of the word "Introducing." The left-
hand page was its mirror image in reverse. In the center of
the O was, against the severe black and white, a four-color
photograph of the Speedfoam box. No pitch; no copy; nothing
else.

"Thanks. Four or five or ten more won't hurt. They like to
think you've bled a little." It only occurred to him a second
later that "they" could be read as he. Somehow he had never
quite gotten used to being Management.

Rapidly blocking in the third of the morning's layouts, he

thought idly that Saturday ought to be a good day for the viper. Desk drawers, inevitably left unlocked by some, to be opened and pried into; new secrets to be discovered if they were not already known to this faceless man or woman. A key might be used for entrance—there was nothing to say that it wasn't an executive with a hidden streak of the nut in him— or merely a ring of the bell, and, "Hello, Mr. Poll, work to do, isn't it ghastly?" Did Poll keep any written record of who came in to work on weekends? Ask Watters. Make a *note* to ask Watters, otherwise he'd forget about it. He was for some reason back in Anne's hall.

Like a neighborhood dog barking and setting off a chorus of his fellows, the mynah bird's "Good news!" had swept Anne's aviary into vocal action. Coos and whistles and chirps, and from the parrot a resounding, "Tally me bananas!" The heart-melting music pouring down the stairs. And Bridget in her robe, clean innocent smell of soap around her.

"Good morning, Mr. Cavanaugh," Watters said in the open doorway. "Shame to put *you* to work on a weekend. I have hot coffee on a ring in my office, care for a cup?"

Did Watters always work on weekends, one of those men bound by umbilical cord to their places of employment? As though hearing the unspoken question, Watters went on, "As far as anyone's concerned I'm not officially here. Just, as it were, an invisible eye or ear. In case that bitch or bastard"— the two designations somehow, from him, startlingly ugly— "shows up to leave a note or so around."

Kells said thoughtfully, "Thanks, no coffee." Watters, with a little duck of his head, silently disappeared.

TWELVE

In bed in her flat on South Audley Street, Mrs. Cleat found sleep evading her; or rather she was evading it, she admitted. There were so many delightful things to think about, relish, chew upon.

She felt like Jove with lightning bolts in her fist, or in a more contemporary sense like a combat soldier pondering when exactly to unpin a grenade and throw it with maximum results.

Facts. The more the better, although she already had the one big glorious fact. *Caro darling, 24 Emlyn Court.*

But, when he had entered Rooks Mews he was intact, splendid as always. When he had come out, the streetlight briefly showed that he had been marked. Bandaged. Hit, or hurt, preferably both. By whom, and why? It was pleasant to think of someone inflicting bodily injury upon Ian Milford.

She had been wise to put up with it, to stay, to force down the daily drink of acid, put her pride away to keep in her office safe, knowing it couldn't go on forever, not with the Montroy bitch. She could, of course, have left, there were a dozen firms who would have snapped her up. But twenty years of her life had gone into Pruitt and Cream and it was her territory, her place, her own land.

Two o'clock. She turned on her other side and gave her pillow a hearty punch. She was the only occupant of the double bed. Cyril Cleat had perished under a Number 14 bus nine years ago, in his shortsighted progress through a rainy November night. But this was in a way a posthumous death. His wife had consumed and digested him long before it. He had been a stockbroker making a quietly comfortable income.

"Really, my dear, it's not necessary that you work any longer," he had said to his wife shortly after their marriage. She informed him that her work was her life. "Oh well then, all right, if that's what you want to do, my dear."

She rose as always at six. Saturday and Sunday were the busiest days of the week at Pruitt and Cream. Nominally she had any two other days off at her own choosing but she seldom took them. On the weekend, however, the office did not open until eleven.

She marched into the bathroom and had her usual one-minute hot, three-minute ice cold shower. She did her knee bends and toe-touchings and deep breathing at the open bedroom window for exactly fifteen minutes. Her breakfast consisted of cold cereal, which she crunched busily, and decaffeinated instant coffee, followed by an orange eaten section by section. The white outer flesh so good for one. Then a B-complex vitamin tablet with a large glass of water.

While she was forcing her way into her large girdle, she found reasons to approve her small-hours plan to investigate Rooks Mews. There might be some charming property hidden away, unexpected, unseen, in the mews. She had for years made a practice of tracking places down, places not yet for sale, and putting their descriptions in a file which she labeled "Who Knows?"

And, she could walk at least part of the way. Her ankle was much improved. Ten blocks or so, bracing. The best of all physical exercise after the age of forty, doctors said, and it didn't cost one a cent.

Besides, who in Rooks Mews had taken a swipe at Ian Milford?

To allow for that bad habit so many people had, sleeping late on Saturday, she did a quick tidy of the flat and tried to devote her attention to *The Times,* picked up off the doormat. Jessica Montroy might be back, let's see, the day after tomorrow, or Michaelmas, or Christmas, there was no way of know-

ing. It might be a good plan to call Lord Montroy and find
out if and when she was expected. But a little waiting, a putting off of the feast for the famished, wouldn't hurt.

How delightful it would be to drop a word or so, to let him
know that she knew. What would he do? A dangerous
delight, perhaps; but she was good at taking care of herself.

At nine-twenty, she walked briskly along Mount Street to
Park Lane. She gave her legs a good hard workout in Hyde
Park, then emerged at the Albert Memorial onto Kensington
Gore, where she boarded a bus.

It was four minutes of ten when she entered Rooks Mews.
She had occasion later to remember the exact time.

The mews was disappointing in a way, and in a way not.
The one house, attractive, narrowed things down. The shop-
fronted warehouse widened things up again. There might be
squads of people employed inside, one of whom might have
injured Ian Milford. But did he consort with ordinary working people? Unlikely.

She moved first toward the pale blue house in its bouquet
of willow branches. The door was a few inches open. Well, a
nice morning, the occupant might be airing away last night's
cigarette or cigar or marijuana smoke. The house looked like
a good candidate for her "Who Knows?" list. She knocked
briskly at the door, waited a full minute, and heard only the
ticking of a clock which must be quite near, inside.

Ravenous curiosity made her push the door wide enough
open to admit her bulk. She had it ready on her tongue,
"What a charming house, I'm told it may be for sale," and so
on and so forth.

A man lay on the hall floor, facedown. He wore well-
polished brown boots, smoke-green corduroy trousers, and a
white shirt with deeper green stripes. The back of the shirt
had a great red-black blotch on it. The man lay very still. It
was a proclaiming and final stillness that hit Mrs. Cleat like a
blast of wind and sound. He was beyond any reasonable
doubt dead, the man here in the hall.

A gun lay near his right hand, black, dull-shiny, its only

purpose in existence achieved. Extinction. Death. And blood released from the containing veins.

The living, working long-case clock ticked firmly on, as though nothing at all had happened several feet away from its glowing mahogany inlaid with satinwood.

From somewhere near, outside the door, a man's voice hailed, "Hi, Peter! Just going to open up. I've brought you a prune puff for breakfast."

Mrs. Cleat had made no sound except for the first harsh stunned gasp, but now she turned and screamed as the man pulled the door wide open and stood framed in light that glistened on his bald head. He seemed to stand there forever, looking down at the floor.

After a time he moved past Mrs. Cleat and went down on one knee near the man's shoulder. Shiny brown hair the man had, spilling carelessly forward. He touched the hand that lay near the gun, and then snatched his fingers away as though the cold flesh had burned them. He stood up again, slowly. Tears began to run down his face.

"Well, that's that, isn't it," he said. He took out a handkerchief and swabbed his cheeks. He let out a long sighing breath.

Then his eyes fastened on her. He took a menacing step forward. "Who are you and what are you doing here?"

With a shaking hand she found one of her cards and gave it to him. "I only just got here. . . . I'd heard the house might be for sale. . . . The door was a little open and I thought I'd put my head in and give a shout, I thought with the door open there must be somebody at home. And then I . . ." Her throat would not produce another syllable.

The long-case clock looked crooked and the body on the floor seemed to rise a little. She leaned hard against the edge of the desk and grasped a corner of it. I have never fainted in my life, I will not faint now. She was vaguely aware of the man's moving through a doorway into a room outside her field of vision.

The sounds of a telephone being dialed and then the words, as though heard echoing down a tunnel. ". . . Yes, dead. Yes, absolutely sure. Shot. Peter Queen. Rooks Mews, it's just south of— Oh, you know it? Good. My name is Hans Baum. Yes, of course I'll remain."

Silence. Mrs. Cleat wanted to go and see where he was and what he was doing but for the moment she was unable to trust her knees and leave the support of the desk. For the first time fear for herself swept hot and cold over her. What if he had done it?

And what if he had gone out the back door? Of course there would be one, probably from the kitchen. Approaching the house, she had caught a glimpse of a corner of a small bricked garden behind it. What if he was circling the house now, to come back in again, close the door, and deal with the only other person who knew this man was dead?

She called loudly, "I think I will go along now, you have my card if I am needed for—" No, don't say for what. It felt strange to make an announcement about a business card in what might be an empty house. She made a tentative, braced half turn to the front door.

Then a light whish which must be a swinging kitchen door. He came back into the hall with a small paper cup. "Here's a bit of brandy for you, I don't want you passing out on top of him." He took her card out of his pocket and glanced at it. "Pruitt and Cream—Ian's place. I don't get it. Did he tell you this house is for sale? Did he send you here this morning? Is this some kind of plan you two have worked out?" He looked dangerous in a very real sense.

She summoned a matching belligerence. "This was entirely my idea, the house. And it is *not* Ian's place. He is merely an agent, or salesman, just as I am. We work entirely separately, thank God." She drank her brandy. "I will be at that address most of the day if I am wanted."

"Are you crazy? You found him, you're the first one the police will want to talk to." With a kind of exhausted, noncaring malice, he added, "They might even wonder if you came back to see if he really was dead, people sometimes do worry about that, afterward."

"If you must jabber nonsense, can't we get out of this *hall*," Mrs. Cleat cried. "Away from—" She stalked past him into the room on the right, a small sitting room washed in willow-waving sunlight. Turning, she said, "I didn't know him, never saw him before, hadn't heard his name until you gave it over the telephone just now."

"Tell that and anything else up your sleeve to the proper authorities," Hans Baum said over the near sound of the police car hooter.

"A what, a *picnic*, Caroline?" Ian asked as though not quite believing his ears.

"Yes, the three of us, after Markie gets back from his ride. It ought to be lovely on the downs, and it's a family thing to do, and fun."

It was close on noon. Ian in his country-gentleman clothes was standing at one of the long windows of the library, a drink in his hand.

"Besides, you look pale and all wound up after the week in town. It's much healthier drinking hot tea in the open air than whiskey in the house."

"Ants in the cheese, and grasshoppers down inside my shirt collar—no thank you." At her little pout of disappointment and the faint flush of a strong will crossed, he went over and kissed her. "Actually, darling, I'm waiting for an important call. My sort of business doesn't stop on weekends. Take Mark to your favorite ant and grasshopper station and have a nice motherly time with him."

Up close, she noticed the beads of sweat just below his hairline and the taut pallor at his nostril corners. "But is this a crisis call of some kind? Business needn't be all that important to you any longer, you know."

"No, just a—" He turned away and went and got his glass from the mantelpiece. "I won't bore you with it, but it is important." He looked at his watch. "I should have had it before now."

Mrs. Burris, Anne's obliging one-woman skeleton staff when she spent the occasional weekend at Alton Hall, seemed almost to have heard her cue to walk on stage. From the door, she said, "Telephone for you, Mr. Milford, will you take it in there?"

Caroline showed no disposition to move, but instead was watching him anxiously.

"No—or, yes, all right."

It was Hans Baum. "Hello, Ian. Something's happened which may or may not be news to you."

Ian interrupted him. "What the hell do you mean, may or may not be?"

"But you haven't even heard what it is yet, hold your horses." The voice was grim, with a glinting knife-edge to it. "Peter's been done. He's dead. Shot through the heart. From behind."

At the thrown-back head and half-closed eyes, Caroline rushed to put an arm around his shoulders.

She would be able to hear Hans Baum.

"In his own hall. With his own gun. Found this morning by, you may be interested to hear, a woman from your office, a Mrs. Cleat. Of course the most obvious thing is attempted robbery, he went after the villains with his gun and they took it away from him. But why then in his own house? You'd think in those circumstances he'd be found in the warehouse. Clumsy job all told. Or over-hasty."

Caroline heard "gun" and "villains" and "found." The look on Ian's face terrified her. She tightened her arm about him and took the receiver from his hand. "Look," she said, "I don't know who you are but Mr. Milford has had an awful shock. He'll call you back, he's not able to speak right this minute. Give me your number, please."

"He knows it. Queen's Taste."

"Till later, then." Caroline replaced the receiver with a crash. "Your drink's right by your hand, darling, take a good gulp. And sit down." Concerned, puzzled, she asked, "But I don't . . . Is that the call you were waiting for?"

"Christ, no! That was about a plantation in Barbados—"

The phone rang again. He picked it up before she could and covered the mouthpiece with his palm. "Caroline, there are things you wouldn't want to hear the odds and ends of—if rough for me, worse for you. Will you—?"

"Of course." She left the room and closed the door.

"I got your number from your office," Hans said. "Are you selling or buying in Sussex, or what? When did you go down there? Last night or this morning?"

"I'm with friends," Ian said. He had left no name or address, only the number or numbers demanded by Pruitt and Cream from its personnel on weekends. "But yes, I was expecting an office call here." Caroline, it occurred to him, might be listening outside the door, worrying about her dear shattered Ian. "Drove down this morning." He very much disliked being on the wrong end of questions and answers.

"When did it happen? Or don't they know yet?"

"Round about midnight, if a smashed watch is to be believed."

"I can't tell you how appalled I am, Hans. As a matter of fact I haven't quite taken it in yet."

"You will. The whole thing. By the way, the police wanted a list of his friends and associates. Naturally I couldn't leave you out."

"Naturally," Ian agreed, steadying to the menace in the other man's voice. "A friend as old and close as I am. And for that matter as you are. I assume neither of us is going to let Peter down, not now."

"You mean farther down than six feet deep or the end of the slide in the crematorium? It's every man for himself, I'd say, from here on in."

In an attempt to compose his face and give the furious, mirrored red of it some time to subside, Ian went to the window and stood very still with his hands in his pockets, his back to the room. Stay away, Caroline, leave me alone for a bit.

The library was in the two-story center block of the stone house and looked out on a circle of shadowed grass. To the left and right curved the graceful crescent wings, like open arms extended for an embrace. Alton Hall was now and then included in books of architecture as a charming curiosity. Anne's great-great-grandfather had been fond of London crescents and saw no reason why he couldn't have crescents in the country.

There was a great peacefulness of trees beyond the grass and flanking the house, immense old beeches, their thinning leaves moving a little in a light wind. The property was tucked into a sweeping dimple on the downs, a hundred acres of it. It would in time be inherited by Mrs. Ian Milford. Along with the house in town. Along with—

To say nothing of Mrs. Ian Milford's own income, and the principal from which it flowed.

It would be a lot to lose.

Mentally, he heard the police knuckles on the front door. Nonsense. But it was time to get back into his skin, back into the country weekend with his future wife and her child and her aunt, the life of the privileged, the invulnerable.

"Found . . . by a woman from your office, a Mrs. Cleat."

It was so mad that he had been holding it, unexamined, at the back of his head. But coincidences of the most unbelievable kind did happen, and all the time. Queen's Taste did a reasonably good retail business, prices perhaps a third below what you'd pay at Harrods or Liberty or Selfridges. Maybe the woman had a wedding present to spring for and wanted to save a few pounds on it.

Don't think about it because there is absolutely no rhyme or reason to Mrs. Cleat's having come upon the body of Peter Queen in his front hall.

Yes, just shopping. That had to be it. Hans didn't open Queen's Taste until ten. Maybe a knock at Peter's door to ask when opening time was.

But Peter couldn't have answered the door. Not if he was dead.

Could the door, unnoticed, have been left a little open?

Don't think about it.

Stop.

Get out of the house and find more air to breathe, away from the enclosing walls and the telephone and a door to be knocked upon with official thunder.

Anne, who was expecting her neighbor Major Farrell for lunch, said in the kitchen, "A good idea, all that fresh air for Markie."

Caroline was slicing cucumbers for the picnic sandwiches. Eggs were hard-cooking themselves in boiled water in a covered pot. "May we take the chocolate cake or is that for dinner? Poor Ian's terribly upset and this may help take his mind off it."

"Upset about what?"

Caroline repeated word for word what he had told her when finally he came out of the library. An old acquaintance —he'd more or less lost touch with him but saw him occasionally—had died very suddenly. The police weren't sure yet whether it was deliberate homicide or a robbery mess-up. The man was in the import-export business, or had been last Ian heard. And he wished there was something he could do but couldn't think what. He supposed the funeral would be sometime early in the week, Monday perhaps; he'd be back in time for that.

She didn't add his closing sentences, which had brought tears to her eyes. "Yes, let's have a picnic after all. I need to be away and alone with my family."

THIRTEEN

Even if the lovers had not wanted privacy, it was provided in generous quantity by Markie. Being with them, just the two of them, embarrassed him deeply, over and above his dislike and fear of Ian.

After he had eaten one hard-boiled egg and a pear, he scrambled up off the plaid blanket and said he was going to look for butterflies.

(For a moment, for shelter, he was back on the downs on a summer afternoon with Bridget. The lovely winged thing had settled on a nearby head of pink clover and he had asked, "What kind is it, do you know, Bridget?" And had giggled when she said, "That is the Great Devonshire Spotted Cavanaugh.")

"But you won't find any at this time of the year, darling," Caroline said.

"I'll look anyway."

"Well, no farther than those trees up there on top of the hill, where I can still see you."

The stand of willows was comfortably far away from Ian's yellow sweater and heather tweed trousers; Ian's long strong hand folding over his mother's forearm; Ian's silvery-gold hair gleaming like metal in the sun.

"His back's to me, I can now thank God kiss you," Ian said, and did, lingeringly and with what she thought was an understandable touch of desperation. "Wednesday sounds right to me, does it to you?"

He had been within limits tolerant of Caroline's apparently arbitrary choice of mid-October for their marriage. It made perfect sense to her but she chose not to explain the reasons. Her father had died on the first of October three years ago and it seemed not quite the thing to marry close to that date. And, she and Kells had been married on the sixth of October. Bad luck to be a few days before or after the anniversary of that wedding. A third consideration, which she admitted to herself might be thought silly by some, was that by the fifteenth she would have known Ian exactly four months. Marrying after four months appeared to her to be somehow more sedate and selective than after three, or three and a half.

"Let's see, Wednesday is the twelfth. Saturday, I think, darling. That would suit me much better. And then there's your . . . funeral to go to early in the week."

Funeral. Horrid dank dark word under this finely polished high blue sky.

His face shadowed and hardened. "Yes, all right. Saturday it is." He kissed her again. How brilliant his eyes were, close, intent. "One week. D'you suppose your bloody Kells will want to be best man or something?"

Caroline was not offended; what she took to be visceral, possessive jealousy warmed her. "Oh, I should think we'd be well rid of him by then. His threshold of boredom is terribly low."

Mrs. Cleat from the police point of view was an excellent witness, factual and crisp, without interruptive sniffles and "oh dears" or exclamations of distress and horror. She did, however, stay firmly with her fictional reason for entering the house. "In my line of work I am an inveterate house-gazer, you never know what treasure you may come upon, tucked away out of sight." As she looked the sort of woman to boldly shove a stranger's door open, her subsequent discovery of the body raised no obvious questions. Particularly as Hans Baum put her in the clear, more or less.

"I never saw her before. And I don't think he'd have made a recent friend of her—who'd chum up, he least of all, with an armored tank? I could swear she didn't know who he was. Alive or, Christ, dead."

It crossed the inspector's mind that the pair of them could have fixed something up. I don't know her, she doesn't know me. On the surface it seemed unlikely, and in any case he hoped for something simpler—a woman, say. Or a burglary at the warehouse. Burglaries were on his mind as he had just closed a case in Camden Town where a night watchman had been killed in a distributing warehouse full of ladies' shoes.

After her interview Mrs. Cleat, upon supplying her home address and telephone number, was allowed to go on her way. The question as to where she had been the night before was, at least right now, a formality and she recognized it as such. She had gone straight home from work and soaked her slightly twisted ankle in hot water, she reported, and then after cooking her dinner had gone to bed early with her book.

She saw no reason to offer the police Ian Milford and his marked cheek. It would muddy the waters of her story if it didn't implicate her outright. And she wanted it for herself anyway, for the time being. For her Ian dossier.

But. What if he had gone back there, later?

Bold as she was, Mrs. Cleat felt a shrinking inside her. He would know, soon, that she had been there and found the dead man. It would probably all appear in the newspapers, if Peter Queen's sudden death was colorful enough in the opinion of the press to give space to. Well, just stick to the house-shopping story, hell or high water.

People didn't go around murdering other people in multiples. Unless they were obsessed, or mad. And Ian struck her as coldly and solidly sane.

In the tall yellow house on Park Lane, she unlocked the office door to the maddening ringing of a telephone which silenced itself half a second before she could pick it up. Eleven-seventeen. God knows how many buyers and sellers had been lost in the seventeen minutes, or given good reason to doubt the efficiency of Pruitt and Cream. Dorothy was off today, but would be on tomorrow.

Now that she was here and able to attend to things the telephone was for a while mute. She felt suddenly shaky and a little hysterical after the control she had exhibited in the morning.

The green-and-white shirt with the great awful blotch on it. The pink bald head of that man Baum, bent close over the silky brown-haired head.

She tried to busy herself typing up a mouth-watering description of the girl Margaret Graves' aunt's property in Cornwall. She studied the drawing of the house front, the paper looking a little yellowed with age but the drawing charming. Keep it for herself, this one, even though the girl had so rudely said she had wanted Ian Milford to handle it for her.

The telephone did finally ring at twelve. It was Hans Baum, wanting to know where he could get in touch with Ian; he wasn't at home in Chelsea Cloisters. Could Mrs. Cleat assist him?

Then he did have some kind of connection with that man on the floor; Baum no doubt wanted to inform him about the death. If, that is, Ian didn't know about it already.

She went to look at Dorothy's book and found the Sussex number, no name, no address. What if he wasn't there at all, just wanted to place himself conveniently out of town—on paper—and out of the immediate reach of the police?

She was sorely tempted to call the number herself, and see. But it wouldn't do if he himself answered the phone. A little too much, hunting him down a few hours after she had found Peter Queen. Whom until this morning she hadn't even known existed.

Odd, that. He didn't exist anymore.

Brusquely, she passed along the number, feeling that in some way she might be actually conspiring with Ian, backing him up, helping him out.

The phone rang again almost immediately. The voice gave her a severe jolt.

"*Can* you for God's sake tell me where Ian is to be found?" Impatient, impolite, nothing new about that.

"Oh, then you're back, Lady Jessica?"

"Yes." The syllable made it clear that Mrs. Cleat didn't rate an explanation for an earlier return from Greece than expected. "Don't staff usually leave weekend numbers?"

Staff. How her fancy man would love that. She ached to pass along her Emlyn Court information, but not now, certainly not in person. Too genuinely dangerous. "Mrs. Cleat told me that you . . ." on the same day the same Mrs. Cleat had found a man dead.

"Yes, I have it here." Reluctantly, she read off the number.

If Mrs. Cleat had been clear sailing on a short run, Peter Queen's assistant was another matter. His red eyes, his tight grief showed strong emotional involvement of one kind or another. Complicated and opaque.

Baum told the C.I.D. inspector, Carling, that he had been in Queen's employ for nine years. Here at the warehouse, at Queen's Taste? No, since their days in Salisbury, Rhodesia, where Queen had also been in the import-export business.

It seemed a waste of time to ask why the two of them had left Rhodesia but Carling asked it anyway. He made a small quick note to check with the police there if it became necessary.

"For God's sake, Inspector," Baum answered him, "haven't you looked at television for the past few years?"

As they talked. Carling tried without much success to place him, docket him. Nothing servile in his manner but no rasp of assertive independence either. He seemed young for a head so glossily, totally bald. Jeans, but clean and well-cut, pale blue shirt open at the neck, old but handsome jacket of brandy-colored Spanish leather. Holding himself rigidly together, except for the eyes, under what had obviously been a very bad blow indeed.

Now then, the woman. Was Queen married? Divorced? Living with anyone, having an on-and-off affair with anyone? He had been married and then divorced, six months later, ten years ago in Salisbury, Baum said. And no, he didn't know of any girl Peter was particularly friendly with at the moment.

Even so, men sometimes had casual companions during the night hours. While the technical squad was at work in the hall, a swift search was made of the little two-story house. It appeared to be an entirely male establishment. The bed had not been slept in or on. The bedroom closet was full of expensive men's clothing. There was nothing there to indicate the presence of the female, no blot of lipstick on a tossed-away tissue, no alien hair to be seen in the immaculate silver-backed brushes, no lingering memory of scent. (And nothing to signal the intimate presence of a male companion, either.)

On getting the report of the search, Carling sighed. A woman, or say a lover, a quarrel, shot with his own gun by her or by the man—how delightfully simple for the police if not for the deceased. And a great savings in taxpayers' money poured out on an extended investigation.

Did Baum know where the gun was kept? Yes, in the drawer in the hall desk. Peter had pointed that out to him in case of an emergency at the shop or the warehouse. Was the drawer kept locked? "No—who'd want to find a key and work a lock with a thug breathing down your neck?"

If not a lover—and not Baum—what about a burglary?

When the two crossed the yard to the shop, the lock of the door was found intact. Baum opened it with his key. Then they checked the only other entrance, at the loading platform. It too looked untinkered with. The mews gate was not locked at night but merely latched. "He always said what's the point," Baum explained. "Anyone who wanted to get in could climb up the ivy and over the wall. And as you know a hot wire disposes of broken bottles in no time." There was, he added, a burglar alarm system installed in the warehouse. "Your people would have a record if it had gone off, wouldn't they?"

The warehouse itself was divided into a rambling series of high-ceilinged dusty rooms furnished with an infinity of boxes and cartons and cylinders, some stacked, some leaning against walls, some large as coffins and some even larger. "You can see," Baum pointed out, "it could take me—or someone—days to find if any of this stuff's been fiddled with."

Carling mentally groaned. He was aware of the traps awaiting him when he went into the question of an aborted—or who knew, perhaps a successful?—robbery at the warehouse. For tax purposes, there could easily be two sets of books and two inventory lists.

In an oddly vague and unwilling way, Baum offered a theory. "It's my idea they never got in here. Peter might have seen them from the house and shouted at them to get the hell away. They could have rushed him and gotten the gun away from him. Some kind of fight—Peter was tough, you know— but then in the end . . ." His voice had been dropping steadily and ended up in close to a whisper.

Carling wanted to know if Peter owned the premises outright or had Baum or any other person an interest or share in Queen's Taste? No, it was all his, Baum said. His and the bank's, that is.

And had Baum any idea who Queen's heir was? "No, his answer to the word will was, won't. But then, who'd blame him for that? He was young, to die. I suppose what he has, or had, will fall into Her Majesty's lap."

A preliminary on-the-spot examination of the body placed the probable time of death at somewhere between 11 P.M. and 1 A.M. Peter Queen's wristwatch had helpfully smashed itself at twelve-ten.

Baum's statement of his own whereabouts the night before had yet to be checked: he had been at a friend's house near Putney Heath until two in the morning. They had been playing poker. He gave three names. After he left he had driven himself home in his Ford Cortina, arriving at his flat in Bayswater at twenty minutes to three.

When, yesterday evening, had he left the warehouse? Same as always, he locked up at six-thirty. Had Peter Queen been home then? Yes, he thought so. Had there been anyone with him? Was he expecting a visitor or visitors? Come to that, did

Baum know of anyone he might be doing battle with in a business or personal way, anyone who might have some reason to want to harm him?

They were sitting now in the small untidy office behind the shop, Carling occupying the desk chair and Baum facing. Baum looked past the inspector's head at shelves stacked with account books and spindled order forms and the usual toppling, choking tide of paper that went with doing any kind of business today. His large blue eyes were fixed and staring. He opened his mouth and then closed it again. A faint ripple seemed to run over the skin of his face and neck. Delayed shock?

"No," he said. "No one. No one that I know of, that is."

Major Farrell was a harmless widower whose large landholdings lay next to Anne's. She had owed him a return lunch for four months and had remembered a favorite dish of his, fresh pineapple sticks wrapped in grilled ham and served on asparagus with a creamy cheese sauce. They were consuming this with pleasure and sipping a rosé when the telephone rang in the hall.

"Damn," said Anne.

"Hideous instrument," Major Farrell agreed.

Mrs. Burris, not having been warned until the evening before of the weekend project, was out doing some auxiliary meat and grocery shopping. Anne went to the telephone.

A woman's voice, not bothering to identify itself, said, "I'm trying to reach Ian Milford. Is he there?"

"Yes, but out on the downs, I believe."

"Looking over the property then?"

Anne found herself a little confused by this. "I would imagine so, it's rather a fine day. . . ."

"Do you by any chance know his schedule?"

What schedule? "Well . . . we'll be here until Monday morning, unless for some reason he has to be in town early Monday."

"*Can* you give me your name and address please. It's rather urgent."

Anne did so, and it was only after the curt thank-you that she thought how odd it was that the caller had not then proceeded to give her name, or any number at which Ian could call her back. If it was really so urgent . . . ?

Going back to her food and Major Farrell, Anne reported, "A woman wanting Ian Milford, who's staying here with us." For some reason she didn't want to tell him that Ian and Caroline were going to be married; it made it more official, final and real. "The strangest thing . . ." She frowned a little, hearing again the commanding, to-hell-with-you voice, "She reminded me of my father."

FOURTEEN

Scotland Yard lost no time in releasing the story. Carling did the briefing in the press room. There was always the beautiful remote hope that a citizen would come forward and say, "I happened to be passing by the gate of Rooks Mews at twelve-fifteen last night and a man came out with blood spattered all over his raincoat. Here is his exact description."

The mews was not overlooked; its neighboring buildings on either side were just about the height of the brick wall around the yard. The only tall building was three blocks away and unless some voyeur had been busily scanning lighted windows with his binoculars, it was a waste of time.

Patient plodding, patient questions to occupants of dwellings near the mews produced little. Several people had heard a loud report around midnight and thought it was a car or truck backfiring. An elderly woman said she heard what to her was obviously a gun being discharged, but she had just taken a sleeping pill, and was frightened, and merely put in her wax ear stopples. To complicate matters, there was a retired colonel on Lever's Lane who loathed cats. He had bought himself a toy pistol and was in the habit of firing blanks out the window when neighborhood cats disturbed his rest. He had, it turned out, been indignantly reported to the police three times during the past two years, and had been duly admonished not to continue this practice, sir, it Constitutes a Public Nuisance. The colonel said when questioned that he hadn't fired away at any bloody cats last night, but was not necessarily to be believed in this assertion.

Queen's Taste could have done a thriving business that afternoon. The usual collection of the curious kept arriving and departing after gazing at the street sign, the ivy, and the brick walk. The premises, however, were sealed and guarded front and back, and Queen's Taste wouldn't be open on Sunday anyway, so there was no chance to get close to the gory scene.

Hans Baum was allowed to return to his flat on the understanding that he was not to leave the city without informing the police as to his intended whereabouts. His attendance at the Putney Heath poker party had been verified by the three other players, all men, whose names he had given; as well as his two-o'clock departure from the house. It was conceivable that one man would cover for another man. But hardly three, and moderately respectable types at that: a manager of a dry-cleaning establishment, a men's wear buyer at Selfridges, and the host, who owned a small Italian restaurant in Bayswater where Hans, who frequented it, had met him.

It had been years since he had had a Saturday off. He fought the temptation to go to the Grapes and Thistles nearby and get numbingly drunk. Justified, in the face of this bereavement. But he had better, from this hour on, keep his wits about him. He settled for a pint of lager and a cheese and chutney sandwich at a pub he'd never been in before, about halfway home on his walk to his flat.

He had some hard thinking to do, some plans as vague and dark as distant drifting storm clouds to pin down and channel. "It's my idea they never got in here. Peter might have seen them from the house and . . ." He smiled bitterly to himself.

It's not as simple as that, Ian. It doesn't really matter what *they* settle for. You know it and I know it. Now, I suppose, yes, it's a weary question of who gets who first.

"You," Ben Voight said, "are a layout factory. I think you have earned a bottle of bitter. I just happen to have two of same in my coat pockets. Will you join me?"

"I will," said Kells. "I think I'm ready to toss in my felt-tips." He got up, stretched, and yawned, and heard the pleasant sound down the hall of bottle caps being pried off.

His telephone, on a nights-and-weekends direct line, rang.

It was Gerald, on the attack. "I hope for God's sake I'm to expect you back Monday, I'm up to my ass in Lola-Cola, in fact
damned near drowning in it."

"Certainly not Monday. Put Ingrid on it, she's really very
good, and she likes working all night. I suppose it has something to do with the midnight sun."

"What are you doing, waiting around for this Milford man
to commit a felony or something?"

As it would have been impossible to describe what he was
doing about Ian Milford (so far it could be summed up in a
word as nothing), he gave an indirect answer. "Chasing a
loose end here and there. And I've seen very little of Markie.
He's in the country for the weekend."

"Country," growled Gerald. "*Weekend*. I think you like the
pace over there. It suits you to put your feet up and muse.
Well, if you're later than Wednesday I will hold you strictly
responsible for the loss of the account. If we do lose it. Oh
Christ, all right—Jenny wants to send you a kiss over the
phone."

Ben came in with seven layouts, the bitter, and two pewter
mugs. Kells had barely managed a thirsty pull when the telephone rang again.

"It might," Ben said modestly, "be for me. Oh, hello,
Maisie. Yes, he's here, all twelve cylinders of him ticking over.
Come and join us, we've settled down to drinking." He
handed the receiver to Kells.

"Don't panic," Maisie said, "and maybe it has nothing to do
with anything. But it was on the news—on the radio—that
Peter Queen has been killed. The Swallow. You remember?"

Four or five seconds later she said in a small reminding
voice, "Kells?"

Peter Queen, who just yesterday had found out something
Ian Milford didn't want him to know. Found out that he was
going to marry Caroline.

No connection. Of course not.

Too bad about Queen though.

He recovered his breath. "Killed . . . you mean in a car accident, or—?"

"No. Frightful melodramatic word but I suppose it's correct here: murdered. Shot through the back. With a gun."

"I think," he said, "I'd better come over right away. You're at home?"

"Yes. And do."

"Are you all right?" Ben asked. "What kind of thunderbolt did she toss at you?"

Kells didn't want to explain because putting it all into words would be impossible, and if possible would sound ridiculous. "A Maisie emergency," he said.

Ben looked surly for a moment. "First my office and now the girl I lust after. Oh well, you've finished our weekend work and it's only ten after one. Don't do anything I wouldn't do. Thanks very much, Kells," with a deep bow at the wall of layouts.

Walking was not to be considered. Kells found himself in a hurry he didn't quite understand. He waved down a taxi at the corner of Allory Place and said, "Twenty-four Emlyn Court." He didn't apprehend himself saying it and was at first indignant and then a little appalled when the taxi bore him straight to Chelsea.

A mistake natural enough under the circumstances. His subconscious must have told him to see Bridget first and foremost. She might slam the door on the dark unknown passageway. No, Kells, no connection whatever, this matter of Peter Queen.

There was no answer to the knocker nor after its three thumps to the bell. She couldn't be having a second bath, she must be out. Strange and unreasonable that you always thought she would be there when she was needed.

Not exactly thinking, but moving as though someone had a hand at the small of his back, pushing him, he decided it wouldn't hurt to take a look at the neighborhood pubs. She could be anywhere, miles away. Or she could be right around this corner, or the next one up ahead.

Not really an irrational pursuit, this: if he found a welcoming pub, he could use a gin and lemon, double. Here on Pelham Street, memory flashed a message. "They have the most divine grilled sandwiches," Caroline said. "It's a pet place, everybody you know is there."

Bridget was there. In a little booth tucked into a corner, profile to him, a man across the table from her. A Bridget on holiday, joltingly unfamiliar, slender olive-green trousers suit, gold flashing at her wrist, dark hair swinging forward as she bent her head in private laughter. The man was laughing too. Squarish, looking seated to be middle height, blunt open face, tawny red hair. And, alertly inquiring glance going to the door when Kells entered, beacon-blue eyes.

Well, go ahead and interrupt them, don't just stand here. He walked to the booth and said, "Hello, Bridget." She made a sudden surprised move of her hand that almost spilled her drink. "Oh—hello, Kells. Kells Cavanaugh, David McEvoy. Will you join us?"

McEvoy stood up and shook hands with vivid hostility. "Come on, Cavanaugh, it's the help's day off." His smile didn't soften it. Kells felt himself being measured, studied, weighed, with speed and intensity. As though this assessment was of considerable personal importance to the other man.

"I know, and I'm sorry, but I will join you for exactly five minutes by the clock. Or under. Bridget, are you ready for another?" And if you want another, you can get it for yourself, McEvoy.

"Yes, please," Bridget said, breath sounding a little spent. "Thomas Powers."

He went to the bar and got her Irish whiskey and his gin and lemon. He plucked an unoccupied red leather stool from the end of the next booth and sat down on it. Addressing Bridget, he asked, "Do you know someone named Peter Queen?"

"The late Peter Queen," McEvoy corrected. "Rooks Mews. Bullet through the heart. Queen's Folly, or some such name, shop and warehouse, burglary the first poss. Why should Bridget know this unfortunate corpse?"

"I don't," Bridget said, looking puzzled. "I don't know the man but for some reason I know the name. Poor man!"

"Would you have heard it from Milford?" Kells pressed.

"Or maybe you've just heard it on the news—radio, television—"

"No, I was giving myself a vacation today from the world I live in—" She turned a deep pink. "I'm sorry, I didn't mean that the way it sounded. It's an odd name, isn't it?" Her eyes took on an inward-gazing look as she searched for the reference.

"You'd have to be very sure of yourself—one way or the other—to keep a name like that," McEvoy said.

"I connect it with Markie. Something he said, something he heard, I don't know where—and did he make a nonsense rhyme of it . . . ?"

Very bad; cold, icy bad; but probably nothing, Kells told himself. A child's fascination with certain sounds, certain words, which became verbal playthings.

Bridget looked at him in amazement. Was it her imagination or had he shivered for part of a second? She studied the narrow face which wore as a rule its own light of wit and intelligence. Closed now, darkened. He was there but he had gone away, far away.

My own darling. My love. If I could put my arms around you, you mightn't be so chilled and frightened.

Now, what on earth kind of mad train of thought was this?

But keep your eyes down, eyes tell tales. She looked into her glass, lifted it slowly, and took a sip of the soft golden Powers. Kells stood up. "If you remember the rhyme, Bridget, and I don't see how you could, will you save it for me?" He paused, and then quoted to her, " 'There is something of the night about him.' "

She said hotly, "That's even more below the belt now than it was then. I wasn't thinking what I was saying."

"Oh. Well, nice to have met you, McEvoy." And he was gone.

"I don't see the link between daddy and your little darling and this chap who fielded a bullet," David said. "And, come to think, he mentioned Milford too."

"Don't look for a link, at least not on your typewriter. It's unfair to all concerned, and there wasn't time to tell him you work for a newspaper."

"I'll try not to if you'll come back to me, Bridget."

"From where?"

"From him."

"You can't come back when you've never left," Bridget assured him serenely.

Maisie lived in one of two small apartments on the second floor of a carriage house on Farm Street. Small, but it had a railed balcony full of fresh growing things, the blessing of a great plane tree, and a wall of mirror facing the balcony which doubled the splendor of the tree. It also had, now, a tiny kitten of a beautiful deep gray. Maisie had for some time wanted a Siamese, but it was against her principles to bypass animal shelters where dogs and cats waited hopefully and then often hopelessly in cages. She had adopted the kitten at eleven this morning. No, no charge, miss, but if you'd care to make a contribution—Maisie had whipped out a ten-pound note. She was in no time attached to the kitten, whom she named Casey. If Kells got it, his own initials, well, all right—in a roundabout way he had been responsible for her new friend.

When he arrived at her door, he put his arms around her and kissed her, not with passion but with great affection, and mainly for his own comfort. He was immediately attacked by a guilt that did not explain itself.

"Mmmm," Maisie murmured. "You feel lovely. You look worried. But then, it is peculiar, isn't it? The very day after you met him."

"Irrational is more the word for the shape I'm in. I've invented this vision of Queen saying to Milford, 'But you can't get married, you're married already. No wonder you kept it a secret.' And Milford reaching for the nearest gun. While the meanest intelligence would see at once there is no connection whatever."

For God's sake stop talking, sounding like a hysterical fool.

He saw himself with distaste in the mirror wall, a shadowy stalking man in a gray suit that looked in this light funeral-black. Beyond him, from the balcony, an innocent blaze of pink and scarlet geraniums and a snowfall of white petunias. Maisie watching him, eyes very wide, but then they were always like that.

A memory of Gerald, scolding, came back to the man in the mirror. "I *think* my way step by step to a conclusion. You just take a careless flying leap through the air and land squarely on it. It's not," Gerald continued complainingly, "what I would call fair." He had, of course, been talking about advertising problems.

"But," Kells said, to Gerald or himself or Maisie, he wasn't sure which, "this isn't a hamlet with a handful of people in it. This is the city of London. How many millions? And Queen looked like a man who gets around. There would certainly be dozens of . . ." He found himself lacking either the conviction or the energy to complete this sentence. "But Markie ran across him somewhere or heard his name or— And I wish to Christ he hadn't."

Maisie had vanished from the mirror but then reappeared in it with two wineglasses full of gin and lemon. "I've been listening all the time but I thought these were sorely needed. Stop prowling and sit down. Give me your free hand and I'll warm it for you. *I've* heard of all sorts of ghastly people but that doesn't mean I'll ever have any contact of any kind with them."

She had, she said, called everybody she knew to see if they knew anybody who had it in for Peter. "Nobody knew a damned thing."

Round face close to his, she backtracked a little. "You're not worried. You're terrified."

Either fight it off—the dreadful, the grotesque possibility—or face it somehow, meet it, and take it from there.

"Yes," said Kells. "I am."

FIFTEEN

It was nominally her wedding anniversary that brought Jessica Montroy back from Greece several weeks earlier than she had originally planned (insofar as she could ever be said to plan anything). But she had a growing hunger for Ian along with a mounting suspicion of what he might be up to in her absence. She had called him six times in the past month, nights and weekends, and had only gotten him once. In a wild hurry, he said, on his way to an appointment. With what or whom? A house to show or a woman's waiting body?

High time to get him back on the leash. Besides, she had accomplished her purpose in going to Greece to stay with the Pendletons on their idly cruising yacht. One morning in early September, she woke and examined herself naked, slowly and severely, from head to foot, in her dressing-room cheval glass. She had had a rather rackety year, late nights and drink and Ian, and it was beginning to show on her prized flesh. Oh God, look at the eye pouches. And, call a spade a spade, the belly. Skin color all wrong, yellowish. Even her hair had lost its spring and bounce and was lightless.

She decided at once on a private and personal health cure. The Pendletons' invitation was a standing one. For a month, she took the most devoted care of herself. She drank nothing but champagne and not very much of that, swam a great deal, sunned, creamed and lotioned, and did a daily hour of her ballet exercises in the yacht's small but well-equipped gymnasium. She ate, sparingly, lean meat and salads and fruit and gave herself nine hours of sleep every night.

It worked. So well that Jules Pendleton had to be forcibly

ejected from her bedroom—it was too roomy and elegant to be called a cabin—at two o'clock one morning. All right then, Jessica thought, what am I doing here while Ian may be busily plucking roses in London? She had deliberately not thought often about him, just concentrated on getting around to looking terrific again. Her willpower was formidable, if she said so herself. But now she wanted him, a good strong dose of him.

It would be fun, nice savage fun, to slither down to Sussex and see what, exactly, he was doing there. The woman who had answered the phone had said *we'll* be here until Monday morning. An educated, moneyed voice but not young; and Ian in her view hadn't yet reached the point where he had to peddle himself to older women. Another thing, he didn't like the country, it bored him. He was in her word a townie to his bones. Was there someone else included in "we"? Female?

But no blazing hurry. He'd be there, at Alton Hall, until Sunday night. He was a sitting duck.

She had a late lunch with her old friend Annie Wormsley, and caught up with all the gossip, and allowed herself the suspended pleasure of three powerful martinis before buckling down to her deviled breast of chicken.

Among other items, Annie told her that Peter Queen had been, can you believe it, flat-out murdered. "Weird word when you say it. But that's the word the BBC man used." Yes, found at his house today. "I remember meeting him once with you and Ian, that mad night in Pimlico, the name stuck with me."

"Have they any idea yet who did it?" Jessica asked with brilliant interest.

"Not according to the last news. I suppose some boring thugs wanting to get at his import-export goodies."

"I don't know," Jessica said slowly. "I've an idea that he was up to some kind of dangerous fiddle on the side. It's annoying that you can't always remember clearly things you catch when you're drunk. Perhaps it will come back to me if I work on it."

She crunched a piece of thin cheese toast and asked in a careless way, and without consciously meaning to make any kind of connection, "Have you seen Ian around?"

"No. But—such a welter of phone calls this morning— Hugh saw him just last night. At the Connaught Grill. Dining with a man and a woman, very pretty she was, Hugh said. He thought they, the couple, were Americans but wasn't sure."

Well, couple. That sounded all right. Two men, one woman. Ian didn't ordinarily believe in sharing.

Her car was brought to Annie's door at three. It was a custom-built Gaspard, available only to the very rich, and Jessica loved it dearly. Long fawn body, wire-wheel spare tire in a recessed mount on its left front fender. Jade-green glove leather upholstery, dashboard of winy brown ship's teak, and the sweeping overall grace of a sea gull floating down to land on the beach. She liked driving it fast but thought this was not the time to be stopped and made to take a breath test. Any kind of summons (short of homicide, she qualified) could be handled and disposed of, but it would be a bore to have to blow into their peeping-tom device.

With the top down and her hair wind-tossed, she drove south through Surrey and into Sussex. She stopped only once, at Cuckfield, at a pub called the Cowbells. Her martinis had made her thirsty and she downed a pint of bitter. Quick trip to the ladies' and then, Here I come, Ian.

The ivy-scrawled wooden gate in the long stone wall was hospitably wide open. A long curving tree-bordered drive within. Good. It might be wise to leave her car some distance from the house and approach on foot. Ian might spot the Gaspard and have time to hide whoever the rest of "we" was in a closet. If indeed there was such a person.

She stopped the car under a beech tree and got out. Something made her look up and she saw a small boy perched on a bough three feet above her head, legs dangling, one hand clasping the tree trunk and the other holding a half-eaten apple.

"That's a pretty car," he said.

"Isn't it? *Do* you like it? *Who* are you?"

He liked the car but thought instantly that he didn't particularly like her. She reminded him of Ian but how could she? She was a woman.

"Mark Cavanaugh." He didn't mind "Mark" when he said it himself, to a stranger.

"Not Eldredge, then."

"No, that's my aunt. Great-aunt, I think."

How nice, to have an information service right here, out of sight of the house.

"And Mr. Milford, Ian, is staying the weekend with you and your aunt?"

"Not really with us," Markie said. "Or yes, well, I suppose so."

"Then with who?"

"With my mother."

"And who might your mother be?"

"Her name is—" As he never himself used it, there was a flicker of hesitation, "Caroline. Caroline Cavanaugh."

"Caroline," Jessica said in a testing fashion. "Now, do I know her? Are she and Ian old friends?"

"Not so old. They're going to be married though."

A leaf detached itself somewhere high above, brushed the healing scab on Markie's knee, and landed in Jessica's blown black hair.

"They are? When?" Her voice was light and controlled but something about her eyes frightened him a little. He let go of his apple and it hit the ground.

"I don't know if I should be talking about them to you," he said, but politely. "I don't know who you are."

Might as well get it all. Drink it to the sour dregs while the drinking was good. Or available.

"Come now, you must have heard my name." She found a smile. "Jessica. I'm a family friend from away back." No specifying which, whose, or what family. "And your own father?" With a blurred idea of wanting to strike out and return hurt, "Is he dead?"

"No," flamed Markie. "*No!*" He addressed this to her and to the tree and the sky and to forever and ever. "They're divorced."

The probably American couple with Ian at the Connaught, and Hugh thinking the woman was so pretty. Yes.

"Lovely news about the wedding. When is it to be?"

"Next . . . Saturday." He was looking at the toe of his sandal and his voice, reluctantly producing the words, was just above a whisper. And you don't like it either, Jessica thought.

"Well, I'll leave the car here and pop up to the house." It hadn't been, after all, nice to offer him the death of his father. "Would you like to sit at the wheel and pretend you're driving it?"

"Thank you but I think I'll just stay here," Markie said, "until tea." She saw that he was trembling. Best to leave him alone. Perhaps children, like cats, healed themselves.

She walked steadily up the drive. The house revealed itself around the next curve. Very nice, Ian. Money here. But that's more or less your line, isn't it? You wouldn't develop a sudden overwhelming passion for a woman with a regular balance of a hundred or so in Barclay's Bank.

She crossed the grass between the welcoming arms of the crescent wings. Almost twilight here, but late low sun was tangled in the softly moving branches of the trees. She knocked firmly on the oak door.

"I'll get it," Caroline called to the kitchen, where Mrs. Burris was busy with tea preparations. Anne was in her bath, she presumed. Ian had gone out an hour before with one of Anne's father's collection of guns. "I might pot at a rook or two and see if my aim's still good," he had said. She approved of this manly, English way to take air and exercise before tea; and somehow she felt sure Ian's aim would be very good.

Not, in this amiable house, cautious about people wanting admittance, she opened the door and saw the tall, lean, and rather beautiful woman. *If* you liked the type, thought Caroline in a second's summing up.

"Yes?"

"Are you Caroline Cavanaugh?"

Jessica had for her part returned the swift all-inclusive examination.

Soft and slender, a shine about her, happiness or maybe she had been born that way. Long loose dress, creamy silk, smocked at the shoulders. Lighted blue eyes, gleaming brown hair. Blessed Damozel look, Jessica put it to herself.

"Yes, I am," Caroline said. The woman's crisp confidence made her add, "Is it Anne you're after? Do come in. She ought to be out of her bath soon."

"Thank you. I'm Jessica Montroy." She came into the hall and then through the folded-back pale green doors into the drawing room. She took off her leather gloves and thrust them into her pocket and went to the fire to hold out her hands. She turned around in a leisurely way to face Caroline.

"Actually I'm not here to see Anne Eldredge. You happen to have something of mine here. I've come to collect it."

"Something of yours?" She must, Caroline decided, have been a guest here recently and left a raincoat, or an umbrella, or perhaps a piece of jewelry forgotten in a dresser drawer.

"A man. Ian Milford." The leisurely air vanished. Jessica looked and was savage. "Or didn't you know?"

After a stretched silence, Caroline asked in a cresting voice, "Didn't I know *what*? If you're not here to see Anne, and as I don't know you, I think you had better leave, immediately."

"There couldn't be two Ian Milfords, could there?" Jessica sat down on the arm of a chair near the fire. "One hundred and eighty pounds, last I heard. Or felt. The best twenty-four-karat hair. Small mole on his left buttock. Such nice *flat* buttocks, don't you find?"

Anne stopped and stood halfway down the stairs, fresh and warm from her bath and now going cold all over.

"Get out of here, you frightful—" Caroline screamed. She had always thought of herself as a gentlewoman under any and all circumstances. This supposition dropped like a garment. "You lying bitch!"

"Where is he, by the way, my Ian?"

"*Prowling dog of a woman he doesn't want*. Obviously."
Caroline raised her voice to a shout. "Mrs. Burris!"

Oh dear, I should go and help, but how? thought Anne.
The other woman sounded terrifying. She would have liked to
run back upstairs but if she stayed silently here she could
catch Markie coming in, and sweep him off to the kitchen, or
the cellar.

"Yes, very much my Ian. Bought and paid for. From his
clothes to his nice little snug at Chelsea Cloisters to his job."

Mrs. Burris appeared nervously in the doorway. "Yes, Mrs.
Cavanaugh?" Her face was scarlet. She had heard what had
just been said about handsome Mr. Milford.

"Show this woman out," Caroline commanded.

"Nonsense, I'm bigger than she is and in perfect combat
condition," Jessica said. "You may go, Mrs. Burris. This is a
private interview."

Caroline picked up a crystal bowl of roses from Anne's embroidery stand and hurled it. Jessica ducked her head and the
bowl smashed, fountaining water and roses, against the edge
of the mantelpiece. Mrs. Burris clutched her apron corners in
her hands and fled to the kitchen.

Without leaving her chair arm, Jessica reached out and
helped herself to the brass-handled poker in its stand on the
hearth.

"You can have him when I've finished with him, but not before," she said. "At the moment he is not, to say the least, free
to marry."

Caroline, panting, advanced across the Aubusson carpet.

"Now look. You might as well take your medicine like a
good girl and calm down. There's rather a nice little child
outside in a tree who might arrive at any second for tea. You
wouldn't want to involve him in this, would you?"

Anne went very quietly down the rest of the stairs and
across the hall and out the front door. If that awful woman
saw her, too bad. She must find Markie, and immediately.

Caroline stopped on the center wreath of the carpet, pink

and ivory roses and looped blue and pale green ribbons. As always, in the rare times when a passion of rage took her, the maddening accompaniment, the enemy, was a pour of tears.

Through her sobbing, she gasped, "Get out . . . get out . . ."

"Good idea. It's just occurred to me Ian may have seen my car and be lurking in the underbrush somewhere. I'll go out and look for him while you recover yourself. But do save a cup of tea for me, I'll be back."

Ian had indeed seen the car and instantly and correctly suspected the worst. Walking up the drive, he also saw Markie in his tree.

Without preamble, he asked, "Did you and she have a chat?"

"She was asking me questions," Markie said coldly and defensively. "She wanted to know what my mother's name was. And when you were going to be married."

"Oh." Ian looked up at him as though he wasn't really there and didn't even exist at all. "I see."

A rifle was cocked over his arm. His father didn't like guns, didn't approve of guns, so neither did Markie.

Ian put a hard hand around his ankle, the fingers sending a message. A threat.

"You haven't seen me. I'm not around. Got it?"

"Yes."

He turned his head and watched Ian moving swiftly between his tree and the next one and down the long steep grassy bank beyond. Then he lowered himself to the ground. It would be nice to be inside, in the house.

Ian took a circular route to the back of the stables. For the past hour he had been exploring the lay of the land; security reasons, he informed himself with a faint smile. And he hadn't then foreseen the arrival of Jessica.

She liked horses. Not a good idea, the stables. The house was out of bounds. She was quite capable of stamping relentlessly through every room of it.

Behind the stables was a small stone building which, Anne said vaguely, she thought might once have been used for making ale. He had earlier noted the half-open window. He gave it a push up, climbed in, and closed the window. The door, he saw, could be locked from the inside. There was only the one nearly bare dusty little room, with a shabby armchair close to the window. And wonder of wonders, on the floor beside it, a half-full bottle of whiskey. This must be the leisure place of the stablehand, who wasn't here today. "I'll saddle Hester for you, Markie," Anne had said this morning. "My stable boy's gone sick."

Normally fastidious, Ian applied his lips without hesitation to the neck of the bottle, seeing no cup or glass to drink from. Then he pulled the chair to a corner which could not be seen by anyone peering in at the window, sat down, placed his gun on the floor beside him, and prepared to wait her out. Not hide, mind you. Just wait her out.

For one of the few times in his life he had no other ideas or alternate plans.

He had been prepared to face her when it was necessary. If she had weapons of attack, so had he. But not here and now. Not in front of Caroline, and Anne. And that kid.

From the door, Mrs. Burris asked timidly, "Shall I serve tea, 'm?" She had seen that woman, that foul-mouthed vixen, go out.

Caroline put a hand to her tear-reddened face. "Bring me a cup in my room, will you, please." Ignominious, but she had to do something about the way she looked. And the door of her room could be locked after her tea came.

She drank it while she washed her face and began to redo her makeup. Just concentrate on this job. Don't, for a little while, think of anything else.

She had gotten to her eyelashes when there was a knock on the bedroom door. "Just me," Mrs. Burris reassured. "She's gone. She left this note on the hall table."

The note said: "Tell Ian I'm sorry but seeing the hour I had to rush back to town—our anniversary party. (Darling Ian, you *are* slippery.) But tell him not to worry. I'll be in immediate touch. J.M."

Markie was coming up the terrace steps when the door opened and Anne said, "Hurry, Markie." She reached down and seized his hand.

"Hurry where?" They were already in motion, almost at a run, around the right-hand crescent.

"I'd forgotten you and I were invited to Major Farrell's for tea," Anne explained breathlessly. In another thirty seconds, they were in the garage, getting into the Bentley.

He was used to her forgetting things but as she was backing out he said, "My hands are dirty, shouldn't I have . . . ?"

"You can wash when we get there." He saw that she was badly shaken and another of the pillars that held him up felt as if it was beginning to sway. Kind absentminded Aunt Anne, a strength always there, in the near background. Never ruffled or flurried about anything, except where she had left her reading glasses, and had anyone seen where she put down her *Martin Chuzzlewit*?

"Is it you that she's a friend of?" he asked, trying to get through to what was worrying her.

"Who?"

"Jessica."

"Oh, is that her name? No." The name and something vaguely familiar about the face came together. That awful Montroy woman. "You can have him when I've finished with him, but not before." She looked capable of anything. "There's rather a nice little child . . . You wouldn't want to involve him in this, would you?"

A terrible battle looming. While she felt in general safer with her own sex, Anne had, sandwiched into sixty years of living, explosive memories of women at war.

"What a delightful surprise," Major Farrell said when the butler led them into his library. Then he must have forgotten too, Markie thought as he was being guided by the butler to the nearest bathroom.

"Trouble at home," Anne said to Major Farrell as she accepted a cup of tea and then put it down because her hands were shaking. "I won't distress you with the details—in fact I think they're in the nature of a family secret—but I must get the boy out. May I use your telephone?"

First, she called Alton Hall and told Mrs. Burris to tell Caroline and only Caroline where she and Markie were. Next, she called the Hyde Park Hotel and was told after persistent ringing of the room number that Mr. Cavanaugh must have gone out, madam.

What *was* the name of his agency? He might be working there. She racked her brains. Oh yes, the same name as his, doubled. A man's voice at the other end said, "No, he left hours ago. No, he didn't leave a number where he could be reached. Sorry."

Now what?

SIXTEEN

In the little stone building which might have been devoted to ale-making, Ian had a great deal to think about and plenty of time to do it.

When darkness fell he could risk exit, approach the house with circumspection, and go in through the kitchen and up the back stairs. The sun was setting now.

Whatever she's been telling you, Caroline darling, is a pack of lies from beginning to end. The fact of the matter is that I turned her down, wouldn't follow her to bed, and she's never forgiven me.

With Caroline, it shouldn't be too difficult.

He helped himself to another swallow of whiskey. Caroline was not, right now, the real problem. She was supremely handleable; she loved him; she would want to be told and shown that she was secure, that Jessica had been what amounted to a brief bad dream.

At least Peter was off his back. Peter in the flesh, that is. "Hmm. Kennet Hall. That rings a bell. He's a collector, or was until he expired. Mind you make me a nice tidy list, Ian."

Strangely enough, they remained friends of a sort. They need offer each other no pretenses. They could be, quite comfortably, what they were, public collars unbuttoned and tie knots loosened.

The risks, Peter pointed out, were all his. "Nothing to connect *you* with a selective heist. You can prove you were somewhere innocently else at the time. They could search your premises and even examine your bank balance. Nothing. You're clean as a whistle." He grinned his fey grin. "In that direction, anyway."

What he was referring to, obliquely, was the sudden death of John Maxford's wife in Salisbury, Rhodesia. Shot through the heart, found a day later in a welter of blood lying half off her bed. As it seemed she had been alone in the handsome isolated house, and no motive offered itself upon investigation, the police reluctantly chalked it up to the random savage work of guerrillas. She had not, however, been raped. The husband was a well-respected man in a firm of house agents. And in any case he had been spending the past few days at the home of a friend in Victoria, where he was handling a piece of property to be disposed of. The friend, Peter Queen, vouched for this. He too was a well-respected young man with a modest import-export business of his own.

There was no overt hurry about their departure from Rhodesia. John Maxford left six months after the death of his wife, and Peter Queen four months after him. At the airport, he had said, "Good-bye but not forever. I'll be in touch with you sooner or later, John." As he had procured new papers, he was familiar with what the new name would be.

They had started their unofficial partnership several years before. There was only one difference in their arrangement there: John Maxford got half the profits realized from untraceable robberies of valuable objects from houses listed with, among other firms, Cane and Cane Ltd.

But that was the past. Now, there was Hans to be dealt with. Unless, prudently, he took to his heels never to be heard of again by the name of Baum. They did marvelous things with wigs these days, hairpieces to be polite. A hairpiece would make a spectacular change in bald Hans. That would be the wisest thing, and what a perfect solution, for the two of them.

And Mrs. Cleat, floating ominously around in the air above his head, had to be tidily buttoned into place. Yes, of course, shopping. Make sure of that, file and forget. But if she hadn't been? Don't count your chickens, don't twist their necks for them, until you knew the hard facts of the matter.

As far as the police went, they would have no way of proving he hadn't been in his place at Chelsea Cloisters all evening and all night. He had summoned the patience to take care that he encounter no one, when he left and when he returned. After living in a place for a while, one gets to know its rhythm, its traffic; which of its stairs and exits are seldom used.

He supposed that as of a little while back he no longer was employed by Pruitt and Cream. Unless she thought she'd fixed it—fixed him, fixed Caroline, and that after a crashing quarrel they could drift back into the status quo.

He was suddenly aware that the window he had been staring at without seeing it had turned dark purple. He slipped out of the door and waited, listening. One wing of the house was dark. But the door to the conservatory in it was usually unlocked until bedtime. Right; it still was. He went through the conservatory, was brushed in the face by a palm frond, and opened the door to the hall a cautious inch.

He heard nothing except a sudden hum and flutter from the fire in the drawing room. He couldn't imagine Jessica being present in this core of domestic silence. Conversely, the silence began to worry him.

Still carrying the gun over his forearm, he crossed the hall, feet soundless on the Indian rug. Then he saw Caroline, sitting, waiting for him, at one end of the sofa.

Oh yes, Christ, the bomb had been dropped all right. Her eyes looked as if she had taken a beating under them.

She asked tonelessly, "Where have you been?"

"Just let me put this gun away." He saw his face in the mirror in the hall and was pleased to note that the palm frond had given his hair a wind-ruffled look. Coming back, he said, "You know how you tease me about being a townie. I got lost. I was following a stream. I think I've been around in several huge circles. And getting dark didn't help."

"Jessica Montroy's been here. She said you belong to her. And a lot of other things."

"*What?* Oh God." And then, "Poor bitch." Ian managed both contempt and weary patience in his voice. "Hell hath no fury like the woman . . . You know the rest of it. She's come into the office several times and screamed this fantasy at me in front of the others. I'd have thrown up the job but she went off on her travels and quiet returned. She thought it would be nice to have me in her bed and I thought it wouldn't. She is, you know, a bit mad. But of course you saw that."

He had rallied all his resources to make this effort. His color was high and spirited, his eyes sparkling. Caroline had never seen him looking more attractive, more desirable. Straight and tall and proud.

"Then it isn't, any of it, true?"

"Not a word, if it's the same script as before." He took a chance, but not a very large one. "About paying my way for me, and other high-handed nonsense." His timing was flawless; he made no attempt to touch her. "Can you, do you really believe that you are not the most important woman, the one woman in the world, to me?"

Caroline's ego, and her passion for him, came rushing to his aid. To have believed Jessica Montroy would have been to lose perhaps forever a great chunk of oneself, one's precious inner self.

How ghastly it must have been for him to be at the mercy of that foul woman. Just because she wanted to get her hands on him and he wasn't having any.

The tears came again, but they were soft and becoming, not the wrench of woe. She rose and went to him and he put his arms around her and very gently kissed her.

Eyes only a few inches from hers, he said, "I don't want, ever, any shadows of any question marks. You're sure you do believe that I stand for truth, and love—and she for the wildest stone-throwing fiction."

"No shadows, ever," Caroline whispered. "I shouldn't have . . . But she was so awful—"

She didn't have to go on with her near-apology. His mouth stopped that.

In this day of what might be considered by some, over-communication, Inspector Bain while reading his evening paper came upon the account of the murder of Peter Queen. He had no information then that his morning's quarry, Ian Milford, had any connection with the violently deceased.

On a thin tip, he had spent most of the day with Liverpool antique dealers, and found nothing to show that in this port city an item or so on his list was waiting quietly, in a back or basement storeroom, to be shipped out.

His nostrils and throat still felt dust-coated. From the kitchen came the scent of oxtail stew, a favorite of his. His wife made it deep-dish fashion, with a thick golden biscuit crust on top. He went to get a glass of lager to chase the dust and, leaning against the counter in the warm kitchen, said to Lucy, "This murder of the import-export man—did you read about it?"

"Yes. Handsome chap in his way."

"It gives me an idea, my seventy-seventh idea by actual count. Wonderful home for stolen goods, import-export places. Repackage, stamp, and ship. To your oil sheiks, or wherever. It would bankrupt Her Majesty's mails to have to open any and every normal-looking shipment going out of this island, containerized or otherwise."

"Mmmm—yes." She opened the oven door, pulled out the rack, and tapped the biscuit crust with her fingernail. "Two more minutes, give you time to get down your beer. But if you've just had an idea, you've also found there's no point in pursuing it."

"Might try one or two of those places, though, on my own. Just a prowl or so. See how they function. Actually, I haven't the foggiest about that particular line of work."

". . . and then he went in and kissed the young woman before closing the door behind him." Don't make it sound too educated, literate; the note was to be anonymous.

She had, earlier in the day, expected by now to be stormed by the press, television cameras included. But Carling informed her he had not given out her name at the briefing. "Might be dangerous for you. After all, we have only your word for how long you were there, and for the moment we accept it. But for all our man knows you might have spotted something, heard something— You are merely described as a house agent who entered the mews because there was a property inside she was interested in acquiring."

A great relief, really, if a bit flattening at first. Now Ian would not read her name in the papers or hear it, or see her face, on the television screen.

Briefly and precisely, she put down her facts. Stronger that way, without embroidery of any sort. She did add the smarmy bit, the overheard telephone conversation: her gloves in his pocket, "all ten delightful fingers of them." Should she add the other business, about Ian's cheek wound acquired about seven hours before Peter Queen was killed? The temptation was powerful. Of course Rooks Mews, and the wound, and the body were an entirely different affair, but they might compose another poisoned arrow to shoot, through Jessica, at Ian. A different affair. She liked the sound of that.

"And now we come to an affair of an entirely different sort." She had typed four more lines when the doorbell rang.

She peered through the eyehole in the door and saw Hans Baum. Backing up a few feet, she called, "Just a minute, please." She went to her bedroom and got her tall rubber rainboots, into one of which she proceeded to put her kitchen meat hammer. It ought to be easy to swing or throw the boot just in case.

Driving curiosity and a desire to continue feeling in the middle of things made it impossible for her to deny him entrance. But when she opened the door her greeting was a suspicious bark. "Yes?"

"I'm not here to check your door number. May I come in?"

Heavens, Mrs. Cleat thought, the man's ten years older than he was this morning. Face hard and grayish, the large blue eyes smaller somehow and without life or light.

"There are things that want talking about."

"That *you* want to talk about, I think you mean. Come in, though, if you must."

She didn't offer to take his coat or ask him to sit down. He walked from her small hall into her sitting room, and swept it with one photographing gaze. He leaned tiredly against her little dining table in the corner.

"You know and I know it wasn't house-hunting that brought you to the mews. The property's on a ten-year leasehold that's only one year old. It suited Peter to a T. He wouldn't have slipped around rumors that he wanted to get rid of it. To Milford or anyone else. And you say you and Milford have nothing to do with each other. Except, of course, working in the same office. So, down the drain with your little story."

"You're not the police!" Mrs. Cleat cried.

"No, but they talk to me quite a lot and will continue to do so. There's a tie here. You and Ian. I'm going to find out what it is before I leave." His eyes were almost mesmerizing now, boring deep into hers. "Hate's as much a bond as friendship. I gather you'd just as soon spit on him as not. What's the connection, Mrs. Cleat?"

She stared at him in pugnacious silence and he went on, "You're endangering yourself, you know."

The boot, with its empty mate, was leaning against the leg of the table beside her. Comforting.

"In what way? By having let you in? If so I'll thank you to leave immediately."

"All right. Guts, that's evident." He even smiled a little. "But you've walked into the middle of a murder. I know you know something, but maybe not enough." He moved, not toward but away from her to the window, with the air of a man collecting his thoughts. She bent, slowly, casually, to pick up the left boot.

As she did, he half turned his head and looked to be brushing lint off his shoulder, a reassuringly commonplace act. His eyes made a lightning scan of the sheet of paper in the typewriter. The top part had flopped over but he caught the last five lines on the roller.

"If you can believe it, I'm trying to help you as well as myself."

"Thank you very much, but I don't want your help." She gestured with the boot. "In fact, I'm just on the point of going out."

Always be firm, never show fear, it might work with people as well as intimidating dogs. It worked now. He sighed and said, "All right, I'm off," and walked to the door. Just before going out, he added, "But don't blame me, Mrs. Cleat, for whatever happens to you."

SEVENTEEN

"Can't I help you, Kells?"

They both knew what Maisie meant. Any kind of help at all, including physical solace, warmth, a loving body, a small sunny place in a darkening wood.

He said slowly, unaware of his accepting and then rejecting face, "Thank you, Maisie dear, but—"

She had given him a sandwich and poured hot strong black coffee into Meissen demitasse cups. She looked closely at her own cup, just now empty, and threw it hard against the mirror wall. A square of mirror shivered into a hundred cracks and with a faint tinkle splinters fell.

"I'm sorry. Bad loser. Go to your dark Rosaleen or whatever her name is."

The telephone beside her rang. It was Ben Voight. Voice a little thick. "Is the phone beside your bed? Is your employer in it? Did I interrupt anything?"

"No to all three. Are you still working?" A minor face-save, Ben's call, but better than none.

"Yes. Trying to prove I'm just as good as he is. I have this terrible temptation to take his whole pile of layouts out to the back court and burn them. No one's seen them but me."

"Don't, Ben."

"Then come and hold my hand, the one I'm not working with, and tell me how great I am." Professionally speaking, Maisie saw it all. Ben at first grateful to Kells for his help, then the gathering resentment and jealousy. A trip to the pub for three or four angry whiskies and probably no lunch. And, grim, back to his board to outdo Kells, come up with a campaign that would blast an entire conference room out of its chairs.

"All right. Say three quarters of an hour."

Kells got to his feet. He knew he had closed a door with force and was sorry, and could find nothing to say. "Thank you for the ear, and the comfort, and lunch, Maisie."

"Are you going to go to him?"

"Who?"

"Markie."

"Yes, I think so. Yes, I have to." He kissed her at the door and went out into the graying afternoon.

If his instincts were right, he had taken a careless thoughtless leap on the lines of Gerald's accusation, and landed on the impossible truth: Ian had killed his friend Peter Queen. Because he formed some kind of immovable impediment to Ian's marriage.

There was no earthly reason to believe that Markie was in any immediate physical danger. Or ever would be. But obviously the marriage could not take place until Queen's death was cleared up, and his killer or killers found. Which might be, Kells well knew, never. How many cases were still open on police books after two, five, ten years?

On the other hand—maybe by tomorrow a solution, maybe this coming week. Headlines flaring, culprit apprehended, Ian entirely innocent. Ian, to whom, mentally, he had done an unforgivable wrong.

He thought about renting a car and decided against it. He'd had a good deal to drink, not that he felt it, but still it was somewhere in his veins. And having had no occasion to drive in England, he didn't fancy learning the left side of the road while caught up in this obsession, unable to concentrate or coordinate. Besides, there was no hurry. And no real reason to worry minute to minute about Markie.

Bridget connected Peter Queen's name with Markie. "Something he said, something he heard, I don't know where."

No, *no*, there wasn't any hurry but he must, for whatever irrational reasons, be there.

He could hardly call Caroline and say, "Send Markie up to me by train, there's a dangerous man in the house with you." The alternative, take the train to Markie.

He went back to the hotel and packed the attaché case Caroline had given him one birthday. Although he wasn't a man to carry papers around, he found it useful for shirt, tie, underwear and toilet things. *Good evening, Anne. I'm to spend Sunday with Lord Streatham and company at Arundel. I don't know how early in the week I'll be leaving for New York, so I thought I'd—* An awkward guest under the circumstances, but Anne would certainly give him a room to sleep in.

Christ, what if Ian took his arrival as an unspoken but naked accusation? Don't think about that. Yes, Lord Streatham, they'll probably expect me to be able to play golf, a bore, especially on Sunday, but that's this business for you. And naturally he'd want to say good-bye to Markie if he had to leave on short notice.

He had a little under an hour until train time.

One plunging insight—if it was that, in the matter of Ian— seemed to have led to another.

It was as though you had been walking along, eyes on the near prosaic ground, and had suddenly been introduced to a mind-rocking view through an observatory telescope. Senses stretched, not only sight but all the rest of them.

Go to your dark Rosaleen.

Bridget was trying without a great deal of success to finish her still life of chrysanthemums. The flowers by now weren't at their freshest, but then neither am I, Bridget thought. She was darkly and obscurely worried about that exchange of words with Kells at the pub—first an unknown dead man discussed and then Kells' quoted reference to Ian.

And worried, too, about what David had said. "Come back

. . . From him." Perhaps it was just as well that Caroline might be trying in a roundabout way to get rid of her. Markie would have to get used to Ian on his own, and better sooner than later.

She resisted a strong desire to get down her suitcase and start packing it. Helter-skeltering wouldn't do; proceed quietly to a normal ending—soon—of a job which had always had an inevitable time limit built into it.

Damn, the telephone. Kells. "Oh good, you're there. I have to stop by for a few minutes to deliver a message. See you in five minutes." Why hadn't he delivered the message over the phone? Oh God, not more about Ian and, what had that man's name been, Queen?

"Peter Queen, a man who's mean, there never was a meaner man than Peter Queen."

Markie's chanted nonsense rhyme had suddenly come back to her, whole. Had he heard Ian use the name, to Caroline or Anne? Surely he had never met the man; she was the willing repository of all his hour-to-hour doings. It must be just the fun of playing with the name.

She was rinsing a sable-tipped brush in water when the knocker sounded. She went down the stairs and opened the door. "Good news!" said the mynah bird. "Come in, Kells," said Bridget.

He took off his raincoat and tossed it over a hall chair. Moving in a deliberate way, he came over to her, put his arms around her, bent and kissed her mouth, at first with an exploring delicacy.

"Kells—" Without attempting to free herself, "Have you forgotten your message?"

"This is the message," he said, and resumed kissing her in freshly discovered passion. Bridget did not mince matters, here and now. She joined him and answered him.

Holding her with the most welcome, warming kind of force, he said after a while, "I was thinking on the way here that I have no surprises left for you. You've seen me sullen, you've seen me drunk, you've sent my rumpled suits to the cleaners and overheard my language at its worst. You've had every chance to study my shortcomings. At close range. And for years."

"There were other things to see, too," Bridget said, dimples faintly denting.

"Then why for God's sake did it take you so long to find out that you were plainly and simply mine?" he demanded, and kissed her again. "No questions asked and no holds barred." He ran a cherishing hand through her dark hair. "*Do* you have any questions?"

"Now . . . no."

"I'd better stop this I suppose—" He dropped one arm to look at his watch.

"Why are you checking the time? Had you made some kind of bet with yourself how long it would take me to topple? Have I lost another stripe?"

He had never before had an opportunity to equate certain moments of love with mirth; but they were shaking with it, joy and laughter, in each other's arms.

"As I remember, Anne usually keeps champagne on ice. Let's go and have some, or I will immediately take you upstairs. And I can't do that because I have a train to catch."

Over the champagne, he told her why he was taking the train.

Bridget's inner-lit face slowly shadowed. "Selfish of me— right now I hate to let the chill, and the world, and Ian, back in to my lovely fireside. But yes, if you feel that way—and I don't *think* you're right, I pray you're not—I don't see what else you can do."

What a dim way to spend Saturday afternoon, Maisie thought as she let herself into the agency with her key. Restoring the ego of a half-sozzled art director. Her own ego could use a little help instead.

How quiet it was here. The elevator was for some mysterious reason padlocked; she took to the stairs. On the third floor, she found Ben Voight peacefully asleep on the sofa in his own large office. Wake him up? No.

She tiptoed to the broad white lacquered table against the opposite wall where there were two stacks of layouts, Kells' instantly recognizable on the right. Would he wake and think again about burning them? At the desk, she wrote a note. "I've put K.C.'s pile in a place beyond temptation. Love your stuff, particularly the one with the rooster in it. Happy dreams. If you're still thirsty I'll be home until seven. M."

She made a neat roll of Kells' work and carrying it silently left the office. If he woke still raging, her own office was the first place he'd look. I am doing this, she told herself, mainly for Ben. He could lose his job over this colorful destructive gesture. Besides, there was something indecent about it; it would be like setting fire to a small but important part of Kells.

Before turning at the banister rail to descend the carpeted flight of stairs, she saw an angled view of the corridor on the second floor. She stopped. Watters was at the closed door of her office. It had been open when she passed it on the way up. What was he doing?

He was taping a piece of scratch-pad paper to the door.

Some seep of fear kept her from doing what she wanted to do, call down to him, "What the hell are you doing, my good man?" He hadn't eyes in his back but he could turn at any second and look up. Even people maintaining perfect silence could send a sort of throb, or tick, through the listening air.

She backed up very slowly until she was out of his range of vision. She pushed open a door to her left, Axel's office, and went in and carefully closed the door behind her. She gave him ten minutes. He'd hardly want to hang around there admiring his handiwork. After all, he was the man in charge of finding the Cavanaugh and Cavanaugh viper.

Correct; the corridor was empty. The note taped to her door said, in block printing: "Maisie's got it made, she's sleeping with the boss. Congratulations from the team. And who did you have to shove out of bed to make room for him, Maisie?"

From the downstairs hall, she heard Mr. Poll say beerily, "Well then, off with you for the day, Mr. Watters?" and the sound of the front door closing.

She pulled the note from the door and put it in her pocket. Safe, now, to continue down to the kitchen, where she proposed to place the roll of layouts in one of the cabinets. She felt a little numb. What an exciting Monday morning that would have made for everybody. Particularly for Kells. Shabby picture, even in these permissive days, leaping hungrily into bed with his just-met employee, Maisie Tombs. How long *had* he been here? Forever. No, three days.

There was, on the polished green-and-white plastic tiling of the kitchen floor, a step behind her. She whirled from the cabinet and Watters said, "I just thought I'd come back and check to see if Voight was awake, wouldn't want him to come to at midnight wondering why he wasn't in his own bed— And then I heard a noise in here."

"Or my bed," Maisie said, forgetting caution in her gush of rage. "When *Mister* Cavanaugh sees fit to leave it vacant. You horrid little man, you."

He leaned and pulled open one of the drawers under the counter and took out a rolling pin. Maisie had a second or so to think, My God, comic strip!

He struck her with it on the side of the head. As she plunged down into the dark empty elevator shaft of unconsciousness, her last flicker of thought was, Oh Kells, oh I wish . . .

Watters reached down and dragged her into the long windowless pantry. He had keys to everything at Cavanaugh and Cavanaugh, and he had a key to this. When parties were given at the agency, the caviar was kept in the small pantry refrigerator to keep it safe from hungry personnel in search of a snack between the writing of print ads or television or radio commercials.

He wiped the hand-held portion of the rolling pin with a

damp piece of paper toweling, went up the stairs, and put it
on the floor beside the sleeping Ben Voight, half under the
sofa skirt. It had a smear of blood on it and several satisfactory pale hairs. He repaired to Maisie's office and on her
desk placed the five-by-seven-inch scratch pad and a pencil.
He put on a glove and started a note.

"To: all and sundry. Did you know, children, that Ben
Voight is bisexual? Let me tell you how I found out. He" and
then the pencil skated sideways as if in the hand of one taken
by surprise.

Ben Voight woke to a second or so of mystification about
what ceiling this was, over his head, and then recalled that
he'd had a lot to drink, and had come back to work and
called Maisie, and while waiting for her had decided to
snatch a nap.

He rolled long-leggedly off the sofa, sat up and rubbed his
eyes and yawned. He did not see the rolling pin but he did
spot a propped-up note against the pencil cup on the desk.
He read it and swore aloud.

Of course he'd never really intended to destroy Cavanaugh's work, had just been amusing himself with the fantasy.
And now, come Monday morning, there would be the question of where it was, and how had the pile been removed
from the big office, and why? The more concern because
Speedfoam was a new product and supposedly secret from
the competition. He could see Watters snooping around, asking questions. Ghastly if the truth, which wasn't the truth at
all, came out. Maisie would be on Kells' side, of course.

He was still a little drunk and found it hard to think
clearly. Well, the obvious thing: go look in her office. He
picked up his coat, feeling that he was in no shape to work.
Perhaps tomorrow.

A minute later he stood looking down at the pad on her
desk. "Did you know, children, that Ben Voight is . . ."

A blaze of fury took him. Why, the little bitch, who would
ever have dreamed—? The first thing he needed was another

drink, and the next, swift revenge. But what to do with the note? It was firm evidence, he couldn't destroy it. Well, if a few people had to see it, that was just too bad. Getting Maisie was more important. Maisie, whom he had wanted for himself. He turned the pad facedown and left it on the desk. Then he ran down the stairs and out the door. Crossing the hall, he thought he heard a distant banging and shouting and put it down to Mr. Poll's television set, in the basement.

At the Private I, he had a quick double scotch and went to the telephone. Cavanaugh ought to know immediately and take appropriate action. Go straight to the top. And incidentally to her current lover.

He was told by the voice at the Hyde Park Hotel that Mr. Cavanaugh was out. Well then, would they take a message for him? An urgent message? Yes indeed, sir.

"I've just found out who our office poison pen is. I believe her full and formal name is Mary Blessington Tombs. I thought you ought to know as soon as possible." He gave his own name and home telephone number. Okay, Maisie, take it from there.

Maisie later figured she must have been out ten minutes or so. Coming to in total darkness, she dismissed the first wild terror of thinking she had lost her sight under the head blow, and recognized the familiar odor of the place, a faint whiff of cheese, a vinegary suggestion of pickles. The pantry off the kitchen, in which there was of course no window.

She pulled herself to her feet, holding on to a cabinet drawer handle, and found the light switch by the door. He hadn't taken her handbag, but then why would he? Her mirror showed blood running down her neck behind her ear, a lot of blood. It had seeped into and along the shoulder of her mauve cashmere pullover. The face in the mirror hazed and the shelves of cans and packages tilted one way, and then the other. For God's sake, not again—

She breathed deeply for a few minutes and the shelves went back to horizontal. Her head still pounding with pain, she tried the doorknob. Locked. She felt in her right-hand pocket. The folded note from her office door wasn't there.

Awful feeling of blood, running. She had no scarf or handkerchief, only paper tissues in her bag. She snatched a six-foot length of paper toweling from the roller and wrapped it as tightly as she could around her neck.

She started out by shouting, "Help. *Help!*" It wouldn't do to begin screaming right away, you might panic and might not be able to stop at all. And it might make the bleeding worse.

She made a quick mental review of the obstacles to her being heard. The pantry door, then the thick baize-covered kitchen door, then the door at the end of the corridor leading past the rest rooms to the entrance hall. Ben, if he was still here, three flights up. Mr. Poll probably in his basement snug, which was at the front. Solid masonry and wood and plaster throughout, offering the natural soundproofing of structural excellence. They don't, Maisie thought, tempted to laugh madly aloud, build them like that anymore.

She began throwing heavy cans of food at the door. Perhaps crashing noises carried better than the human voice. How long did it take you to bleed to death? Would it be wiser to lie on the floor, would that help stop the blood? No, she might pass out again.

But, it occurred to her, he could have killed her outright. The blow had been wild and quick, no considered art to it. It could have caught her on the temple, where the bone was fragile, and— Where would she be right now if he had? There wouldn't be any right now for her, only a forever to inhabit.

A sort of fleeting pity for Watters—poor efficient little mole of a man who must have a sort of cancer of the spirit—vanished, with the knowledge that mild madness could slip several notches and become mortal danger to someone, anyone here. Well, yes, it already had. *Mortal.* Awful, definitive word.

All right, scream, but time the screams by the sweep second

hand of her watch. One every fifteen seconds, four times a minute.

Mr. Poll came and let her out after twelve spaced screams. Through his astonished cluckings, she said, "Watters hit me with a rolling pin and put me in here; I hope he's gone? I caught him planting one of those foul notes."

Mr. Poll's primary concern was finding a place for her to lie down and getting the doctor here as fast as possible, the official company doctor. There might be questions of insurance, a suit against Cavanaugh and Cavanaugh because it happened here on the premises, and God knows what. Besides, the poor girl must be in pain, she looked awful. She was silent now, and meekly lay down on the couch in the ladies' room, a plastic-wrapped pillow under her bleeding head.

Concussed? Mr. Poll wondered, while he waited for Dr. Bender. Or brain all bescrambled just for the moment, and why not, after that whack. Of course it wasn't Mr. Watters, it was Mr. Voight. He had gone up a little while ago to offer him a beer, poor fellow having to work on a Saturday, and found him asleep. He was puzzled about the rolling pin on the floor, with the smear at the end. A prop of some kind, to use in a television commercial? Art directors demanded all kinds of props.

First and foremost, Mr. Cavanaugh must be informed. It was up to him to decide whether to call the police. And then he must try to get hold of Mr. Watters, who would be annoyed if not told what was going on in the office he managed so competently.

EIGHTEEN

Following the principle of the sooner the better, Mrs. Cleat decided to be her own mailman.

She went out into the dark windy evening, refreshing after the long strange day, and made her way on foot to Piccadilly and then down Grosvenor Place to Belgravia. The Montroy house was on Lowndes Street, a little palace of honey-colored stone looking modestly narrow in front but going back and back, to its hidden walled garden. She opened the wrought-iron gate and marched across the paved forecourt to the door, and dropped her letter through the shining brass mail slot. Through a slightly open, tall window to her right, light poured. A man's voice ordered, "champagne over here, and look smart about it. And I counted only eleven vodka, I'll thank you to hand over the other bottle." A party coming up.

Well, you have your party and I'll have mine, Mrs. Cleat thought, trying to envision Jessica Montroy's face when she opened the envelope. Jolting information offered; and in the next paragraph, sweet vengeance offered. *"And now we come to an affair of an entirely different sort."*

She could hear the voice. "D'you suppose their number is still nine-nine-nine?"

She walked back to South Audley Street and on entering the flat thought a little brandy might be a good idea. A flattening fatigue had begun to take over. Check the locks, windows well as the front door and the service entrance. Nice to live in well-patrolled Mayfair.

Let's see, a grilled veal chop for dinner, get out the frozen spinach, and perhaps a tomato halved and broiled? Yes, after another brandy. It was a relief when the ringing of the telephone broke the silence.

Hans Baum said, "Good evening, Mrs. Cleat. You may not think of me as an ally but I am one, of sorts. You'd be wise to get out of there."

"When? And why? What do you mean?"

"Sorry, can't enlarge on it. As to when, as soon as possible. I have an idea you're not safe there."

"But"—more to herself than to him—"where?"

"Keep that to yourself. Don't tell *me*, in case anyone comes to ask about your whereabouts. I'd say you have an hour or so to fade into the landscape."

Fear, which had been waiting in the quiet corners of the room, had urged the checking of doors and windows, came closer. Efficient even as it began to surround her, Mrs. Cleat sat considering. Call Inspector Carling? An understaffed force could hardly supply her with police protection around the clock. Call him anyway.

"Someone's just rung me up and told me to get out of my flat, that I'm in danger here." She didn't name Hans Baum. He had, after all, said he was an ally of sorts.

"Oh. Some normal run of nut, probably, if you know what I mean. We didn't give your name to the press as I told you but it's probably being bandied about Rooks Mews." She was, to put it cold-bloodedly, in no sense a key witness; her evidence was safely in their hands. Wanting attention, perhaps. Unwilling to back off the exciting scene to the familiar dull daily round. "Just be sensible," he said soothingly. "Keep your eye out. And let us know if you get another call."

A hotel? No, she hated hotels and why spend a bundle of perfectly good money on what might be a ridiculous and unnecessary flight? The ideal answer presented itself: the office. Her place, her home, where her real security had always been. She could sleep on the couch in Tony Teller's office. And the staff bathroom when the private house had been converted was allowed to retain its stall shower. She'd be working there tomorrow, anyway.

Ian Milford had never in all the months he'd been with the firm come in on a weekend. Not even in weekend working hours, eleven to five.

It might be interesting to go through his office with an inquiring eye. Letters. And things.

Well, having decided, get on with it. She made a cheese sandwich, filled a thermos bottle with hot tea, and packed her overnight bag. "You have an hour or so. . . ."

There was only a block and a half to walk, up Mount Street to Park Lane, and then another half block.

Jordan, Hans Baum's friend and occasional business associate, was pleased to see her emerge from the front door so soon. The wind was picking up. And, piece of cake, no taxi, just the short walk to Park Lane. Fast on her feet for a stout woman, she was. He saw her into the tall yellow house, waited until lights on the third floor went on, and then went in search of a telephone and a whiskey. The Rose and Crown was just around the corner.

"Thanks, Jordy," Hans Baum said. "Any luggage with her?"

"Small case, as well as her handbag."

"Thanks again."

Luggage, Hans thought, had become quite the style as of the moment. His own well-used case lay open, half packed, on his bed.

Pruitt and Cream. Couldn't be better, really. He hadn't fancied letting her stay in her flat. The man who might be heading her way might worry about the press sniffing out her name and address, wanting a juicy firsthand account from her, camping on her doorstep.

Peter, after all, was an unusually attractive corpse, compared with the ordinary, sordid gray run. Killed in the best of clothing. Shirt, Regent Street. Trousers, Jermyn Street. Boots, St. James Street.

And if the police burrowed deep and long enough, they might come upon Peter's sideline, which would make him an even more interesting story. The sideline in which he had been assisted by a certain Hans Baum. Driving the car, standing watch, helping to lift heavy objects; a two-man job. The police no doubt would plan to put this helpful assistant behind bars. Forget it boys, you're on a dead-cold trail.

He had withdrawn all his money from the bank and emptied his safe deposit box. There was no possibility of an inquiring police ear hearing about this because his banking name was Evan Jones. Meeting his landlady on the staircase earlier, he had told her he was going to spend the rest of the weekend with friends. "Will the police let you?" she asked with avid interest. He was the only one of her boarders who had ever made the TV and the newspapers. "Of course, as long as I don't leave town, they're great at thinking up new questions to ask me about my employer," Hans said.

He took from the bottom drawer of the bureau the box with his new hair in it, a nothing-color brown in a cut between conservative and careless. The box also held a mustache to match, not a burly look-at-me mustache but a rather feeble one; and a pair of cheap Woolworth glasses rimmed in brown. He filled his plastic flask with whiskey and left half a bottle in its usual place on the closet shelf.

If Mrs. Corder, his landlady, chose to examine his room in his absence to see if any bloodied weapon or other thrilling accessories of violence might be concealed in it, she could as he suspected she always did help herself to a nip of whiskey. And if she looked in the bureau drawers and closet would see most of his clothing neatly in place.

He stood looking around for a moment. One way or another, he would never see this room again.

He left his car for good and all at its parking garage, in case the garage had been asked to notify the police if he took it out. It was only an elderly Ford. Employees of small import-export firms did not drive around in Mercedes-Benzes, or Maseratis, if they knew what they were doing.

He took the Underground to Victoria, not only the nearest station but the one for Sussex trains if required. On the way, he returned to his pondering of Mrs. Cleat's typewriter.

Who was she going to send that letter to? The police? It must be going to be anonymous, otherwise she'd stamp into Scotland Yard and denounce Ian in person; much more in character, from what he'd seen of her. It couldn't be *to* Ian, for purposes of extracting money from him; the account of Ian and his actions was in the third person. However, all this was secondary.

In a cubicle in the men's room at Victoria he put on his new hair, his mustache and his glasses. A pocket mirror showed a gratifying change. He didn't look like Hans Baum but he didn't look like someone you'd be interested in looking at either.

He drank a cup of tea at the Buffet just to get used to himself in public and then went to the telephone.

"For you, Mr. Milford," said Mrs. Burris. They must just have been kissing, the two; Caroline moved a discreet foot away from him and touched her hair.

"I'll take it in the library. In case," he added to Caroline, "it's more grue."

He had been on the dangerous brink, a few minutes back, of asking her to marry him tomorrow. He had the license in his billfold. He had persuaded her weeks ago to have it in readiness. "Just in case you change your mind, which I shall work on."

But, no. It could be read as panic, a wild dash into overnight matrimony because something was going to happen, and soon.

And soon.

No. Keep all three oranges in the air, no matter how tired and tense your juggling arm was, for just a little while longer.

Hans Baum's voice on the phone sounded unwilling and even sulky. "I don't know why I'm doing this. But I thought you ought to know. Are you by yourself or do you have your keeper, your girl, listening in?"

"By myself."

"The Cleat female had me a bit worried. I mean, the coincidence of her being there. I don't believe that for a moment, do you?" A bad question, loaded with implications.

"Yes, a bit odd." He didn't trust himself to add any more.

"Anyway, I went to see her. In the course of the visit I spotted a piece of paper in her typewriter. A report of some kind, on you. She's got it all down cold, Ian. She followed you last night. Every step of the way."

Into the silence, he continued, "The only thing I can figure is that she's going to hit you for money. Otherwise why not go straight to the police and tell it to them, not to a piece of paper? I think I made her nervous, going to see her like that. She packed a little bag and took herself off to your house agent's office. Battening down her hatches, I guess. Well, that's it. Forewarned and all that, and I still wonder why I've taken the trouble." The call was abruptly terminated.

Ian felt as if he was falling apart. A deep interior trembling took over. He lifted his hand and looked at it. It didn't show on the outside, that inner shattering, or not yet.

Without any kind of weighing, planning, considering, he went back to the drawing room. "I was right. More grue. Peter's girlfriend is threatening hour to hour to kill herself. One tragedy on top of another—oh God, I must go up to town and talk her out of it."

He was now helped, but didn't know it, by the fact that Caroline had a secret taste for melodrama, especially when it was connected with herself. Kells had never torn off into the night to rescue anyone from suicide. Or been victimized by a stormy titled bitch who wanted but couldn't have him.

"You poor *love*, yes, of course—take the Rover, Anne has the Bentley—I won't hold you, asking silly questions—"

"Where's Mark?" he demanded as he pulled on his trench coat. He couldn't have been there in the library, behind or under something, could he? What had been said on his, Ian's, end of the phone? He had no idea at all.

"With Anne, visiting—tea, I think. Call me and let me know about things as soon as you're able." She kissed him at the door. Poor darling. His lips seemed to be faintly quivering.

Fifteen minutes later, in a day when surprises were beginning to lose their shock value, she heard someone at the door, and Mrs. Burris opening it, and then Kells' voice.

She was eating a belated dinner on a tray table at the drawing-room fire. Heartless, under the circumstances, to have an appetite, but the lamb chops and tomato aspic were delicious.

Although he came quietly enough into the room, the effect was somehow explosive. He dropped his prepared entrance lines. What was Caroline doing alone, with her tray?

"Where's Markie? Where's *Ian?*"

"Markie went off with Anne to tea, now that I think of it they should have been back long ago."

"Tea where? I want to call him and tell him I'm here for the night."

"For the night?" Caroline looked puzzled. "Major Farrell's —the number's on the pad by the phone in the hall. Or, I'll do it, I do wonder why they're so late."

He went and stood beside her while she called. After putting her inquiry, she listened with widening eyes. "Christ, what?" said Kells, reaching out to take the receiver from her. She said, "Thank you, Major Farrell. Good night."

"Anne's taking him back to London," she reported angrily. "They left twenty minutes ago. Do you suppose she's finally round the bend? She told Farrell she'd call me and explain when they got there."

The cold fear in Kells mounted. "Just so I can place everybody—the two of them somewhere on the road, you here—where is Ian?"

"He left for London too—I'd say about a quarter of an hour or so ago." She suddenly didn't want to go into explanations, with him. Murder and now a threat of suicide, not things she wanted to connect in words, to Kells, with Ian.

"Why? I thought he was here for the weekend."

"Something came up," Caroline answered, beginning to feel weary and confused. Anne was a good driver and seldom drank except for an occasional nightcap, but still—

"I must go right back." When he began to know he was frantic, it was maddening to have to invent, to fake. "I only came down to see him; I may have to leave for New York. Is there another car in the garage?"

"No, Ian took the Rover. Kells, what's the *matter* with you?"

I'm half crazy with fear, that's what's the matter with me. Aloud, "I don't want to get back too late and I don't want to wait for a train—is there a car rent place anywhere near?"

"No, not for miles." She gave up trying to understand him. "Let me think. Mrs. Burris' husband runs a sort of taxi service on the side, mostly meeting trains. He might be persuaded to take you up for I'm afraid lots of money."

Within three minutes, negotiations were made over the telephone with Burris, who, recognizing the naked emergency in Kells' voice, said he would drive him to London for fifty pounds. This being agreed upon, he said he'd be at the door in a tick, and was: six minutes.

When Kells urged speed on him, he said, "Fast as we can legally go, sir, and maybe a little faster, but we don't want to end up in the police station, now do we?"

Anne wouldn't have swept Markie away with her unless she had a reason, or thought she had a reason, to be afraid for him.

Just as his father was now, paralyzingly, afraid for him.

Why wasn't Caroline afraid? But then Caroline didn't know.

Didn't know what?

He knew nothing himself, nothing at all, but was just operating on a kind of mad, personal radar.

The radio in the Bentley was on. Anne had a vague terror that there would be an interrupting flash, about an abducted child. Would anyone seeing a black Bentley with the following license number report it at once to the police?

"The French may soon be selling more British lamb to Russia . . . the Gas Corporation is demanding a thirty percent rise in prices for the coming year . . . Scotland Yard is requesting anyone with possibly helpful information on the murder of import-export dealer Peter Queen in Rooks Mews last night to come forward . . ."

Anne was too busy worrying to pay attention to extraneous matters, but the name startled Markie. He was sleepy and bored, and to amuse himself he recited, "Peter Queen, a man who's mean, there never was a meaner man than Peter Queen."

"What's that about, Markie?" Anne asked.

"It's just a funny name. I heard it a long time ago—last month, I think. I was in the wing chair and Ian didn't see me."

"You mustn't eavesdrop," she chided in an automatic fashion.

"It wasn't anything private. Something like, will you please take this message for Peter Queen. And he had to spell out the name, as though the man wasn't a good speller." Markie frowned, concentrating. "The message was 'Dinner party at Dolby tomorrow night.' That was all. That wasn't private, was it?"

Anne, who was not a close reader of the newspapers and whose memory was anything but retentive, could hardly be expected to associate the place name with an account in September of a robbery of French and English antiques from a manor house in Dolby, Wilts.

"No, Markie dear. But still."

NINETEEN

The Montroys' anniversary party was going merrily. It was an open-ended arrangement, people, squads of them, arriving whenever they pleased from seven on. There were two manned drinks tables and a laden fifteen-foot buffet, bowls of caviar at either end. ("I say about two hundred pounds' worth, what do you say?" asked one guest of another.)

Lord Herbert Montroy was as always proud of Jessica, especially so when she was on display in front of a lot of people. She did him credit, did Jessica. Pretty women here, in quantity, but Jessica put them all in the shade. Narrow long black dress with no back to it, cut down in a V to the last vertebra before her buttocks began, high ladylike cowl neck in front. "Amusing, isn't it?" Jessica had said while they were dressing. "I hope it looks as though it cost the earth, because it did." Black billow of hair, eyelash tips painted silver, and a brooch of the Montroy diamonds clipped carelessly at the instep of one of her sleek black satin pumps.

Part of her was enjoying this. Amusing people, most of them friends of hers, with only a few of Herbert's dullards; sociable commotion and gusts of gossip. Another part of her was pouring rage through her veins, rage which demanded to be put to use.

She saw Herbert's secretary, Philip Mott, looking out of his depth in a corner, alone. Herbert had no occupation, but had explained to her long ago that he needed a fellow to answer letters and arrange appointments and pay bills and things.

She went over to him and said, "I want an office cleaned

out tonight, furniture taken away and so on, will you find me someone to do it?"

"Hardly on a *Saturday*, Lady Jessica."

"Screw Saturday," Jessica said. "You're here because you're supposed to be efficient, isn't that right? The faster you find my movers, the better."

He flushed, and then stiff-backed, glass in hand, headed for his office. In the hall, he saw the letter on the floor under the mail drop and picked it up. To Lady Jessica Montroy. Unstamped. She occasionally got signed or unsigned letters denouncing her, after her colorful appearances in the press. They annoyed her greatly. He put it in his pocket to read later before giving it to her. It would be gratifying if it was something especially foul.

Waiting tensely for his return, talking, laughing, seeming entirely herself, Jessica encountered a new experience. Every time she glanced into a mirror, Caroline Cavanaugh's face glanced back at her. The center-parted brown hair, the blue eyes. Eyes, she thought savagely, like blue music.

In twenty minutes Mott came downstairs. He said with evident pleasure, "Because it's Saturday, and last-minute, they will charge you double. White Star Movers, Notting Hill."

"For the double charge, will they go right away?"

Yes; or rather, as soon as they could get hold of their extra man. "And where is it," he asked patiently, "that you want furniture removed from?"

"Pruitt and Cream," Jessica said. "You no doubt have the number on Park Lane. Tell them to empty office number one. Of absolutely everything. I suppose the night watchman keeps keys."

She went and hungrily helped herself to hot toast heaped with caviar. Oh, what fun. Perhaps later she'd dash over there, when the movers had gone. She'd never tried her hand at graffiti. She thought now what a release it must be for all those horrible unlettered people. Write WHORE and TROLLOP and lots of lovely other things all over his office walls, for the staff to see and marvel at. Over their morning tea, on

Monday. Use lipstick? No, not showy enough. Paint and brushes, as she recalled, were standing ready in the storeroom over the garage. The walls would stay that way until the painters were called in to obliterate her graffiti. And there would be plenty of time to get in touch with the press, if she felt like it. What a juicy photograph it would make, Ian's office walls.

Hans Baum had a number of accents at his command. He chose the Scandinavian when he called Scotland Yard. Inspector Carling after a short wait came on. Baum proffered his information and when asked to give his name hung up.

Whatever happened, the next thing to do was get lost. Now that Peter wasn't around, every place was nowhere. Simple: just find another nowhere.

Kells' hands were shaking when he paid Burris his fifty pounds with a ten-pound tip. He went to the door and lifted and dropped the knocker.

Anne opened the door, her book in her hand.

It was like falling down a flight of stairs and landing dazed but unhurt at the bottom. Anne and her welcoming smile and her book. The air of the house bland with peace and security.

"Where's Markie?" But safe and sound, that he knew.

"In bed. The drive made him sleepy. I hope you don't think I'm a nut case, Kells. But that Montroy woman—"

"*What* Montroy woman?"

"Come sit by the fire with me and have a drink, I rather think you need one. And I'll tell you what happened this afternoon."

Remarkably enough, she was not at all vague but brief and crisp.

". . . and then she left, Mrs. Burris told me when I called the house. But she looked to me like a thoroughly unprincipled woman. I didn't know whether she might come back and shoot Ian, or Caroline. Or take Markie as some kind of hostage. Or what. She spoke of Markie in a very unpleasant threatening way. So I just took him. I hope I didn't have you too badly worried."

How warm and bright the fire was, how good his drink tasted. Reprieved, he found himself looking and listening for his love.

But first, there was something to be arranged, or proposed.

He leaned forward. "Anne," he said, "can you say to Caroline that on second thoughts you think she's being hasty? And that if she doesn't wait another six months to marry him you will disinherit her and leave everything to a home for mynah birds?"

"Oh dear, I can't . . ." She blinked. "Yes, I can. *He* thinks I'm a hopeless old ditherer and must have—as a matter of fact I heard him—expressed this opinion to her. You mean, to let this other-woman business to clear itself up."

"Yes." This other-woman business and perhaps this business of murder.

As if to reassure Kells, who had looked so much older a few minutes ago and now mysteriously looked so much younger, she added, "It might persuade. It's quite a lot, my Eldredge bits and pieces."

"Good." He got up. "Where's Bridget?"

"I don't know, upstairs somewhere."

"I'll go and look." He heard her voice before he saw her. The door to Markie's room was a little open. A. A. Milne was being read aloud. "The more it snows, tiddely-pom, the more it snows, tiddely-pom, the more it goes, tiddely-pom, on snowing. The colder my toes, tiddely-pom, the colder my toes, tiddely-pom—"

"*Daddy!*" A shriek of joy from Markie, an eruption of sheets and blanket, a body launched at him, into his arms.

Over his head, Kells asked, "Ian hasn't called or come around?"

"No. Are we to expect him?" Her eyes expressed what her quiet voice couldn't.

"I don't know, now. I'll spend the night here, downstairs on the sofa. Back to bed, Markie, I'll be here in the morning." He spent a three-minute goodnight with his son, Bridget having faded out the door.

He went to her bedroom door and knocked, and spent three more minutes in her arms. "We might as well go and tell Anne," he said.

"Tell her exactly what?"

"That we're a pair."

Bridget glowed softly at him. "All right, Kells." His name, on her lips, like a note in a song.

"And I don't want to frighten her—I'll bed down after she goes to her room."

Anne looked bewildered but inclined to be delighted at their news. "But then of course you've known each other for years—and have been together a great deal of time—" At this, she blushed. Had she implied something indelicate? "But Kells, before I forget, I called your hotel when we got here and was told there were three urgent messages for you."

The Hyde Park Hotel operator sounded glad to unburden herself of all her messages. First, Ben Voight's accusation: the poison pen was Maisie. Second, Mr. Poll's measured statement: the guilty party was Ben Voight, who had when discovered attacked Miss Tombs with a rolling pin. Third, Maisie's own message, which had to it the clear ring of truth. "Ignore Mr. Poll's nonsense, which I overheard while my head was being sponged. It's Watters, the notes, I mean. Don't worry about me, I'm okay."

Must remember tomorrow morning to send Maisie flowers, a lot of them; and gratitude, a lot of that.

But Kells' first reaction was a lateral one. At the moment he didn't give a damn about Watters and his dirty little notes. But if he had been right about Watters—suspecting him instinctively and almost instantly—was he equally correct about Ian?

"You just take a careless flying leap . . ."

It was far too early to think about going to bed, even with a book, even as tired as she was now; not quite seven. Her files had wanted tidying for some time. Mrs. Cleat ate her cheese sandwich, drank her hot tea, and then set to work on the top drawer.

Even when working during the day Saturdays and Sundays she'd never known the office this quiet. It wasn't a business that required late hours. She had almost never been here before at night. Night places have their own, different faces, she thought. And sounds. A very faint dripping from the washroom down the hall—could it be the shower, the water not completely off? Better see to it or it would drive her mad.

To rid herself of an unfamiliar, unpleasant sensation—was it fear?—she invented annoyance. To take the highly questionable word of a total stranger, and leave behind her her comfortable flat, her book, her bath, her bed, because he said he had an idea she wasn't safe there—ridiculous. And what if he had wanted her out of the flat so that he could *himself* get at her in some way? No. He'd told her he didn't want to know where she was going.

It wouldn't hurt to check on the rear door, which led to the stairway. Some careless person might have left it unlocked on Friday.

Who was it she was supposed to be afraid of, and running from? Baum had never mentioned his name. "You've walked into the middle of a murder. I know you know something, but maybe not enough."

A few more lights on would help, even though one did not want to waste energy. They could be turned off when she went to bed. Except perhaps leave the desk lamp on in Tony Teller's office. Like a nursery nightlight, Mrs. Cleat said scoldingly to herself. At your age.

There was no tea left in her thermos and she thought another cup or so might be steadying. Dorothy kept the tin of Earl Grey on the shelf of the coat closet in the reception room. Mrs. Cleat was reaching for it when the door was unlocked and opened.

It was a man she had never seen before, youngish, brown-eyed, well-dressed. Before her shock had time to turn to terror, he said, "It's all right, Mrs.—Cleat, is it? I'm Detective Inspector Warren, C.I.D." He showed her his credentials, and then went swiftly on, "According to information received there may be someone dropping by here we want to talk to. Don't let me bother you. Go on doing whatever you're doing. I'll make myself scarce for the moment. Under no circumstances tell anyone that I'm on the premises."

His voice was educated; he was a reassuring man, quiet and firm. Mrs. Cleat, who didn't like taking orders, was pleased to take his.

Feeling as if she was on stage, but not knowing what play she was appearing in, she went back to her office and made tea on her electric ring. Then she applied herself with vigor to her file drawer. An odd excitement was rising, boiling, inside her ribs.

Not even a cough, a footstep, the pages of a newspaper turning. You'd never know there was anyone else here.

An endless forty minutes or so later, there was a step, at the far end of the corridor. Her tuned-up ears identified the footfalls, coming toward her. She remained in a bending position over the drawer, unable to move her spine or her hands.

In the doorway, Ian said, "Good evening, Mrs. Cleat."

"Good evening." Had the words been able to be heard above the crashing of her heart? Her own ears barely picked them up.

"Working late, I see." Pleasant, polite; although sounding as usual not very interested in her. "As a matter of fact I'm glad to find you here, I wanted to have a word or two with you. Shall we go into my office and make ourselves comfortable?"

He stood back and let her precede him to the large front office. It took all her willpower not to look over her shoulder. He closed the door behind them and waved her to one of the leather armchairs. He took off his trench coat and threw it over the desk, and took the other leather chair.

She couldn't stand the silence, and his powerful silver gaze on her.

"How did you know I would be here?"

"I didn't. I wanted to pick up—" He stopped for a moment and a hard, white fatigue showed on his face. As though an invention, a lie, was suddenly too much trouble. Then he recovered himself. "—a letter that should be answered tomorrow."

"And what did you want to talk to me about?"

"I thought, Mrs. Cleat, I'd give you the opening. As I have observed, you're quite a direct no-nonsense woman."

Don't muff it. Don't turn away from the high hurdle. Don't let this trail off, unspoken, unresolved, so that he would get up and put on his coat and leave. And approach her at another time, when there wasn't a detective inspector on the premises.

The months of hatred took over, intoxicatingly. "Speaking of letters, I've put it all down, about you, at Rooks Mews, going in and coming out with a cheek wound covered up, and then—"

He didn't get up but he leaned forward so that his knees were almost touching hers. His hands hung loosely clasped between them.

"I sent it to Jessica Montroy," she said, face scarlet and heart thudding. "D'you think she'll hush it up for you? Especially as I also told her about your Caroline. At least, I assume Caro is short for Caroline."

"You're a reckless woman," he said. "Do you know that? It *had* occurred to me that it might just be a simple matter of money. I was quite ready to be reasonable, if you were reasonable."

In at the kill. *In at the kill.* The words thundered silently in Mrs. Cleat's head. He'd gone too far. Push him farther.

"As I don't want money, what do you plan to do about me?"

He hadn't taken off his long yellow wool muffler. He did now, whippingly. She struck and kicked at him but he had it around her throat and was in a second behind her. She screamed, a siren sound that was descending into a hoarse gurgle when the door of the office was opened.

There were two uniformed men with Detective Inspector Warren. Each took one of Ian's arms. The sound he made would echo down the years of Mrs. Cleat's lifetime, the rending howl of fury and despair.

"It's all down on tape," Warren said as the air turned quiet. "But from here on in the usual caution applies. It is my duty to inform you that—"

"What the *hell* is going on?" demanded a voice from the doorway. A large burly man stood there, in a dirty blue bib apron over his shirt and trousers. "Shouting and yelling and police—we have orders, anyway, to move the furniture and fittings out of this office."

"You now have orders not to," Warren said. "The office will be sealed as soon as our party takes its leave, which I would say is right now. We'll want you along, Mrs. Cleat, for your statement."

She found herself not wanting to look at Ian. He had sagged forward between the two uniformed men in what must be a faint. She should, she supposed, be feeling a surge of victory. But it wasn't after all a nice place to be: in at the kill.

"It isn't fair," Lucy Bain said indignantly to her husband in the middle of reading the Sunday papers. "Nine months of work for you and then they go and solve it. Not only the robberies but jam and cream on top—a murder."

"*They* didn't solve it," Bain said peaceably. "Ian Milford did it for them."